T0142740

Land ^{of}_{the} Crystal Stars:

Rise of the Guardians'

RIA MATHEWS

authorHOUSE®

Prologue

Once upon a time there was a Majestic Star Kingdom. The kingdom had flourish for many centuries, and it blossomed a whole new light. The star princess was born which brought even more light to the Majestic Star Kingdom. She would rule the kingdom along with her guardians and the elemental prince.

In the kingdom there were parties every night; with dancing, music, and enjoying the peace that the kingdom had offered. There was a Star Princess that lived in this kingdom. She had dark hair, light tan skin, eyes that looked honey when the light would hit them. She was a happy girl, who loved her kingdom and the people in it deeply. Her friends made life as a princess worth wild. The castle was made up of crystal that shined all kinds of colors in the rainbow. The kingdom was peaceful, beautiful, warmth, love, and happiness all around. It had fields upon fields of grass and wildflowers. There are many parks, places to go to enjoy this beauty.

One day she would rule the Majestic Star Kingdom. But she was a girl who also was in love with another. The Star Princess had fallen in love with the prince, who is from the Elemental Star Realm. She would travel to this realm to see the prince; he was dark hair, suntan skin tone, with dark green eyes; with the help of her closest friends. The prince had fallen in love with the Star Princess; and was to protect her with all his might, and The Majestic Star Kingdom.

One day they were to marry; the peace was shattered by an evil that had taken over the Elemental Star Realm. All the other realms; so, anyone from the Elemental Star Realm was suspected to be an enemy; of the Majestic Star Kingdom.

Until one day; the peace was disturbed by an evil that would rule the kingdom; until the Prince and Star Princess could be found again, as this evil had come.

The Queen and King were forced to use their powers to fight the evil. As the fight went on for so many years; it was at that time that the Queen and King could no longer fight against the evil. So, they had to send the prince, princess, and their court a thousand years into the future; hoping there is peace. If the need arises, the twelve guardians could be awakened to protect the world of The Majestic Star Kingdom. As time went on there was children born with special gifts that would lead him and her to be the rightful rulers of the Majestic Star Kingdom.

Chapter 1

⤛⤜⬦⬦⭘⬦⬦⤙⤚

The story begins with finding the twelve guardians so they can be awakened. Each guardian is different and have a power that will help guide the star princess and elemental prince in their journey to rule the worlds. The strongest of the twelve guardians is the guardian of water and ice. Water being a powerful force in nature it can become solid and can turn to a liquid, but it can also destroy.

The first guardian to be found by the protector is the Raven Hair Beauty, which they found on the Crystal Star of Water and Ice Realm. It looks like it rained every day, with beaches, mountains, big and little cities, and towns. When it snowed it would look like the wings of a dove. The glass in the buildings look like ice shining when it rains and snows.

She must be awakened to defend the new Majestic Star Kingdom, which will one day be awaked again and flourish in the future. She will have the powers of the Crystal Star of Water and Ice Realm.

One day the protector seen a girl with hair as

dark as a raven's feather; walking to school, and they sensed strange powers coming from her. They followed her and found that she might be the guardian of the Crystal Star, with powers of water and ice. She watched her all day to see if she might be the one, they are looking for. The girl is in a high school uniform of red and blue. She is known as Alena Patches, age 15, a second former in high school.

"She has to be the one we are looking for" the protector thought. As the protector looked on and study the girl all day while in school. She senses something form the girl; to see if she is the first of the guardians she needed to find.

"I must keep following her, and if the evil comes for her then I will know if she is the first of the 12 guardians." the protector said loud. Then her phone rang, and she answered it after seeing who was calling. "What do you want, or should it be more appropriate what isn't that you know?" the protector asked.

"Have you found a guardian yet? More so have you found her?" the male protector asked on the phone.

"Yes, I found her. We must find and reunite them. Then we shall start looking for our prince and princess. We need them to fight this evil so that we can have peace again." While scratching her head as she answered the other protector on the phone. The protector watched Alena for a few days and followed her to school each day to see if she has the powers of the guardians.

This day was different from any other day the protector followed the guardian to school, but she felt something sinister in the air. Alena went into school as usually, but she even felt that something was off as she enters her homeroom, she saw that there is a new guy in her classroom and new the school as well. She could not help but smile as she looked at him, and he was so handsome that she could not keep her eyes off him. Then something happened that she did not know what o how to think because she felt as if she had met him before in another life or something.

Her best friend Sue Stang came into class after her and saw that she was struck by love at first sight. Sue Stang is a blonde, blue-eyed girl who has known Alena Patches since first grade.

They both became friends instantly "because" both had weird gifts with which they were born. Sue Stang can control light and travel through space, as Alena Patches controls water and ice.

"Who is that boy?" Alena asked.

"That is Leroy Addams. He just transferred here from a far-away country. "Alena, do you like what you see?" Sue said.

"Maybe!" Alena replied

Well as she was thinking, the teacher walks in; and tells the class to take their seats. Alena looks up to see what the teacher writes on the green board with color chalk. She sees that the teacher has put the assignment on the board for the week. It looks like we will be doing an essay on things that matter to us and what we want to be in the future. It must be three pages long with title page, reference page, and an ending. It will be started to finish assignment in no time flat.

"Then she told the new student, go ahead and introduce yourself to the class." The teacher said.

"Hello everyone, my name is Leroy Addams." Leroy said.

"Leroy tells us a little about your-self?" the teacher, Ms. Jones asked.

"Well, I come from a very far-away country that has very little education; and my father had been transferred due to his job." Leroy Addams said.

"Okay, thank you Leroy for introducing your-self and telling everyone a little about you. Ms. Patches could you please show Mr. Addams around school. I do believe that you and Ms. Stang have few classes with him since you three are all in advance classes." Ms. Jones said.

"But Ms. Jones why do I have to show him around? Can another student that is also in advance classes show him around?" Alena asked with a pout.

"Now listen Miss Addams I would ask another student more someone from the student council, but they seem to be busy with school busy and suggested you and Miss Stang to do it because you both are the top two students in the class based on your test scores and your regular class work." Ms. Jones said with anger.

"Mrs. Jones we will be happy to show him around seeing as both Miss Addams and I do have a couple of classes that are different from each other." Sue Stang said with a smile on her face, and she was twisting her blonde hair around her finger. The girls are in the second to last row, while sitting in the back of the classroom they can hear the girls whispering about the new guy.

"Why are they so excited about this guy. They act like we never get new students in here pretty much every year." Alena said under her breathe to no one in particular.

"Oh, do not be so hard on them. They are excited about a new toy. It will fade in time. I don't disagree with them; he is most differently got great looks and if I had to guess a great body too." Sue said with a smile and a dream like eyes while looking at the new guy.

"I do not see it at all. I don't disagree with them either since he is good looking, but there is something ignorant about him." Alena said to Sue.

They smiled at each other and started to giggle. The girls in the back even giggle with them. They can all agree on one thing. That Leroy Addams is most different soft on the eyes and great eye candy even at a distance.

Now class claim down and pay attention and turn to page 356 in your English books. Ms. Jones

"Ha-ha, yes but it was still funny; looking at how red your face got when you saw who had kept you from hitting your nose again. Any way what did your mom pack for you for lunch?" Sue said.

"I won't know until we set down and start to eat our lunch before the bell rings." Alena said.

"Let see what mom made today for my lunch?" Alena was thinking.

"The normal, which is left over from her restaurant, she told Sue." Alena said.

"My lunch is a rice ball, juice, noodles, with some kind of meat." Alena said.

"So, Sue what did your mom make for you today?" Alena asked.

"Well, my mom made me some vegetable stew, a roll, and to drink; my favorite soda; Red Pop." Sue said with a smile.

"Sue, would you like to trade lunches today?" Alena asked.

"Sure" Sue agreed.

She wanted to trade because she wanted what Alena had, because it was by a famous chef; Alena's mother was the best in town.

As the girls ate their lunch; time was moving slow today, and Alena could not get her mind off Leroy for even a second, even though he turned out to be a big fat jerk.

Well as her mind had started to wonder; always at this time of day; the bell rang for their lunch period to end, and the second half of the school day to start. Be finished soon, she had hope that the time will go fast. She was not looking forward to gym for next period with Sue; because she always seemed not to be able to do what the teacher ask of her. Sue was always better at sports than Alena was, but Alena was better at everything else, like schoolwork, test, art, music, and out of all her subjects her most favorite was science class, because she just loved to be outside, even more when they were near water, because it claims her all the time. As it was close to getting to the end of the school day.

"Alena, would you like to go shopping with me after school today?" Sue asked.

"I cannot my mom is expecting me at the restaurant to help set up for the big dinner rush tonight. Sorry Sue tomorrow we can, I will ask her tonight if I can go tomorrow with you." Alena answered.

"Okay" Sue said.

"Well, I will see you after last period." Alena said.

"Okay" Sue said.

As, I walk to my next period; I could not stop from feeling that something was coming or going to happen. Well before, I knew it; I was at my next class, and there sitting in my set was none other than that jerk from lunch "Leroy" talking to those girls that could not stop talking about him since he introduced himself. Well good thing, I only got to put up with him for the rest of the day; because of Science being my last class of the day which hopefully will most differently go fast.

As the time went by, I started to feel as if the world had started to spin, because my mind was full of a dream, I kept having every night for the past month, I had told Sue about it, and asked her "if she has been having some odd dreams lately." Alena's mind was wondering.

She had told me "No. Why?"

Well before I knew it the bell had rang for the day to be over. As, I was walking out the door, Leroy wanted me to walk over to him, and I thought about it, then went against it, and went ahead and left the class with his smile fading from his face, because I was not drooling all over him like other girls were doing. On the way out of the school I see Sue. She was having a polite conversation with someone, but I could not see who it was. Instead of saying bye to her for the day, I just went on home to get ready to go help my mother in the restaurant.

I will see Sue tomorrow at school.

As the protectors watch Alena, they notice that her friend Sue was giving off some strange power as well.

"I wonder if she might be a guardian to." The female protector said.

"Well, she might be the one we are looking for and the Raven Hair Beauty we have seen early, but she is also still putting off some strange powers as well." The male protector said.

"Okay so we might have found two guardians today because of following the Raven Hair Beauty to school today. Now that the day has ended you follow the blonde girl, and I will take the Raven Hair Beauty and see what happens." The female protector said.

"Agreed" said the male protector.

So, the two protectors spilt up to make sure that they might have found two guardians, but still unsure.

When walking home I see someone having some trouble holding onto their groceries, so I went over to see if she might need help.

"Ma'am do you need some help with those groceries?" I asked

"No thank you, young lady, but it was nice of you to offer to help a little old lady." The nice little old lady had said.

Well, I got home changed and went down to the restaurant, running late as always, and it was getting close to the dinner rush. When I finally got to the restaurant something seemed off. I walked through the door of the restaurant and all the workers were out cold.

"I demanded what is going on here?" Alena said.

"Ah; finally, your arrival the first of 12 guardians' that I have been looking for." The mystery person said.

"Again, who are you, and what do you want with me?" Alena said.

"I'm, Morgana, one of many evils to come; to

keep The Majestic Star Kingdom from rising again." Morgana said.

"What are you talking about? What do you mean by The Majestic Star Kingdom?" Alena said.

"You will know soon enough guardian of the Crystal Star that can control water and ice." Morgana said.

"Again, where do you come from? How do you know that?" Alena said.

"I come from the Dark Kingdom Zodiac. You are not the only guardian either; the reason I know who you are is because you are not affected by my spell to control the minds, sprits, souls, and bodies of these mare humans." Morgana said.

"Now my slaves rise and get her." Morgana said.

"NO!!!!!! Someone please HELPS ME!!!!!" Alena yelled.

"Alena listens; you are the guardian of the Crystal Star of water and ice you just have to tape into your powers NOW!!!" the female protector said.

"Who are you? How do you know my name?" Alena asked.

"There is no time to talk about how I know who you are, or who I am. You need to use your powers to defeat Morgana to save your mother and all these people." The female protector said.

"It is too late." Morgana said.

"Dark powers of the Dark Kingdom Zodiac come to me." Morgana said.

"DARK LIGHTNING-BOLT, STRIKE HER WHERE SHE STANDS!" Morgana called.

"Alena, move." Yelled Jennifer the female protector.

"How dare you. You are weak to attack her when she has her back turned to you. You are nothing but a coward." Jennifer said.

"Shield; protect Alena from her attack." The protector called.

"Hahaha. Your shield will not hold against my powers you are weak." Morgana said.

"Thunder strikes the protector!" Morgana called.

"NOOOO; you coward." Alena screamed with anger.

Out of nowhere there shout up a wall of water that started surrounding her. She looked up, down, and around and there is most differently a wall of water protecting her. The water is protecting the protector from the thunder bolt. As Alena looks around the water is not only protecting her and the woman that shouted at her. The water was magnificent with all colors of blues, greens, and teals. It even reminder her of a summer days eve during the summer break. She just looked on with amazement at what is going on. She also cannot believe that she is the one controlling this waterpower. She started to think "where did that come from?" Alena asked herself.

"It came from within you. My name is Jennifer Muse, you can call me Jenny. It is nice to finally meet you guardian of the Crystal Star of Water and Ice." Jennifer said.

Chapter 2

"What do you mean? How can that come from me?" Alena asked.

"Use your powers to stop her in her tracks." Jennifer said.

"How do I do that?" Alena asked.

"You must look deep inside of you. That is where you will find the answer you seek. You will win this battle Guardian of water and ice." The mystery guy said. That came into the restaurant to help defeat this evil. He looked on at the battle and knew that this guardian is very unaware of her powers. He choice to help her no matter what. There was something about this girl that intrigue him both as a classmate and as a guardian. He smiled to himself.

"I will help you." Mystery guy said.

"You can't help her any more than that weak protector Jennifer could not." Morgana said.

"My slaves give me all your energy, to take this guardian out of her miserable life." Morgana said.

"Listen to me guardian, of the Crystal Star of

water and ice. Combine your water attack with my wind attack and we can stop her." Mystery guy said.

"Are you sure it will work to stop her, and save my mother, and all the workers?" Alena asked.

"Yes, you must have trust in yourself, and all your abilities." Mystery guy said.

"Okay, I will." Alena said.

"Then let us begin." Mystery guy said.

"Water come to me." Alena called.

"Wind come to me." Mystery guy called.

"Water Vortex, destroy Morgana." Alena and Mystery guy called.

"I WILL BE BACK for you Alena, guardian of the Crystal Star of Water and Ice." Morgana yelled.

"She will return, and stronger to." Mystery guy said.

"Always believe in yourself Alena, guardian of the Crystal Star of Water and Ice, I will always be here to help you." Mystery guy said.

"Thank you, whoever you maybe." Alena said.

Alena and the Mystery guy had saved everyone including Alena's mother, and the night went on like normal. The only thing that change was that Jennifer stuck around to make sure Alena will be okay, till she went home with her family.

Alena had called Sue the minute she got home to tell her, of the events of the night.

"Sue, I am telling you this man was very handsome, and I meet him before. He was wearing a

Black coat, mask, and black pants." Alena was telling Sue on the phone.

"Alena, are you sure you didn't dream it again?" Sue asked.

"No, it was real, believe me Sue." Alena said.

"Well, Alena if you believe it happened then it happened." Sue said.

"Alena I will talk to you tomorrow at school, meet me in the same place we always do." Sue said.

"Okay." Alena said. Then before she knew it, Alena had fallen asleep, and she was dreaming the most wonderful dream ever.

"The dream was about a kingdom that was so full of life and beauty, every turn you could see millions of flowers so beautiful that all you wanted to do was just lay there, run, and play in this field of flowers in this kingdom. There was someone there waiting for her, it looks like a very handsome guy, that when you looked at him you could tell he was strong, full of life and love." Then her alarm was going off at 7:30am for her to get up and go back to school. But she did not want to wake from the most beautiful dream she had ever had. So, she hit the snooze button and fell back to sleep.

"Alena, get up you are going to be late to school if you don't move it." Alena's mom called.

She woke up and was rushing to get dress and out the door to head to school when she ran into Jennifer getting ready to knock on her front door.

"Mom, can I go shopping today after school with Sue?" Alena asked.

"Yes, you may go Alena." Mom said.

"Mom, I'm leaving for school now, thanks." Alena yelled from the door.

"Bye, Alena, have a wonderful day dear." Mom said.

Alena was walking out of the front door rushing as always because she was running late for school again this morning. As she was running out the front door, she ran into Jennifer Muse.

"What are you doing here?" She asked

"I'm here to make sure we start your training with your waterpower so that we can use it when we need it." Jennifer said.

"Well, can it wait until after school; I'm already running really late for school." Alena said.

On her way to school she was thinking about the dream she had but could not remember what the dream was about. As she was trying to remember, she ran into none other than; "Leroy Addams" coming out of the arcade.

"Hey, watch where you are going." she said.

"Oh, it is only you; Alena, it wasn't me who ran into you, it was you who ran into me, and so you owe me sorry." Leroy said.

"What!" Alena said.

"I did not just come bursting out of the arcade after playing some dumb video games before school, and realized I was running late. So, you owe me the sorry, Mr. I am all that and some more." Alena said.

"You know Alena; you are kind of cute when you are mad." Leroy said.

"Well, you can just keep on walking buddy because I'm not that into you." Alena said.

"You know Alena; you are right, I take back what I said about you being cute. Ha-ha." Leroy said as he was walking down the street laughing so hard you could hear him on the next street over.

"Alena, you are majorly late today." Sue said.

"I'm sorry, I overslept this morning." Alena said.

"By, the way, who were you talking too yesterday after school?" Alena asked.

Sue's face turned so red; you could fry an egg on it. Remembering the conversation, she was having with a certain boy that Alena was secretly crushing on, is not a really good way to be a good friend.

"I was talking to Leroy, after school yesterday." Sue said.

"What!! That jerk." Alena said.

"First off, he isn't a jerk, not me at least, maybe to you because of the way you come off on people sometimes." Sue said with angry.

"I do, not come off like that all the time, just to jerks like him, only after one thing from a girl." Alena said with angry.

"What would that be Alena?" Sue asked

"Don't play dumb, Sue you already know." Alena answered.

"Please, not every guy is like that Alena, and for your information, he was asking how to get to the arcade and the library. So, I told him how to get there and he asked me to come along to show him the way, so I did." Sue said.

"I was trying to be nice to the guy, but if it gets all your buttons into a twist then next time you tell him which way to go when he needs directions to a place Alena." Sue said.

"Maybe I will, if he can stop being a jerk for like two seconds of his life." Alena said.

"Whatever, let's get to class before we are any later then what we already are." Sue said.

"You, know you could have gone ahead without me, Sue." Alena said.

"That is okay, it isn't any fun without you being in class, by the way what you were saying last night about an evil coming." Sue said.

"Never mind about that, I had this amazing dream last night, but I can't seem to remember much about, except for this handsome guy waiting for me and a really big flower field with the most beautiful flowers you could see." Alena said.

"Oh, really, is this a guy I might know about?" Sue asked

"No, I have never met him before." Alena said.

"Well, you are going to have to tell me all about it when you start to remember." Sue said.

As the two friends started walking to their English Class for first period, they notice that a lot of classmates are out of school today. Alena was wondering if it might have anything to do with Morgana that witch from last night; that vowed she would return even stronger than before. I hope this has nothing to do with that evil. I hope it is just some type of flu bug going around Alena was thinking. As class began Alena was hoping that the dream would come back to her so she could tell Sue at lunch today. As time went by things seemed to not be making any sense. How could evil be here, why are they here, what are they after, who are these guardians that must be found. As the bell rand for the period to end, Alena caught up with Sue, to have lunch, but she could not find her.

"Where did she go?" Alena was thinking.

Then she saw her, with none other than Leroy Addams.

"Alena, over here, come have lunch with us?" Sue said.

"I would rather not, thanks anyway Sue." Alena said.

Alena went to her and Sue's favorite spot to eat lunch at, up on the roof top of the school. She felt so betrayed that she could not believe her best friend could choose a boy over her, and not even a good-looking boy at that. Before she knew it Leroy came over to her and started to talk to her.

"Hi, Alena, sorry about yesterday, and this morning. I do not normally act like that around a girl as you." Leroy said.

"What do you want Leroy? Do make it quick I do not have the time for your teasing and bullying today." Alena asked and said.

"I do not want anything. I was just trying to be nice to you now that your best friend is going out with me. Also, when I tease you, it is because I like you as a friend. I do not bully anybody." Leroy said.

"WHAT! You could have fooled me on that note." Alena said.

"Is that true, Sue? How can you go with a guy who teases anyone and everyone he sees'." Alena asked

"Yes, it is true. He is just trying to fit in here since he is new to our school and area." Sue replied.

"You are supposed to be my best friend, and you go and do that." Alena said.

"It is not like you were trying to ask him out and it just happened today when we went and ate our lunch, I wanted you to come along, but you choose not to." Sue whispered.

"Yeah, but you promised you would not ask him out." Alena whispered back.

"It is already done, he asked me to the dance next weekend, and I said yes." Sue said.

"Fine, then go with him." Alena said.

"You, did ask your mom if you can go to the mall with me today, didn't you?" Sue asked.

"Yes, Sue, she said I could go." Alena told her.

"Good, because we have to get the best dresses there is at the mall." Sue said.

"Is, your new boyfriend coming along as well, Sue?" Alena asked.

"Not, sure let me ask him." Sue said.

"Leroy will you be going to the mall with us ladies after school?" Sue asked.

"I will meet you both there after I go home to get some money and stop by the library to return this book I got yesterday." Leroy said.

"That is fine with me." Alena said.

"I'm okay with that handsome." Sue said.

Well as the girls make plans for their shopping day at the mall after school. Alena could not help but be upset with Sue, for asking Leroy out on a date, and most of all to the dance. Well as the day went on it was getting hotter. It just was not normal for this time of the year. Alena started notice that it seemed to feel like summer more than winter. This is clearly not right, when it should be cold outside and not in the high eighty's.

As the school day ended, Alena met up with Sue at their favorite oak tree by the far wall of the school grounds. Sue was waiting and seemed to be very upset about something. Alena walked over to her to see if she was okay. Alena notice that Sue was crying, and she thought that her and Leroy broke up already.

"Sue, what is wrong, why are you crying?" Alena asked.

"It is nothing, just that Leroy said he could not make it after all this afternoon, I wanted you two to get to know each other better so that you two will get along a lot better than you do. I want you two to know each other so that I am not feeling that I must choose between my best friend and my boyfriend." Sue said.

"I am sorry, Sue. I will try and be nicer to him for you." Alena said.

"Thanks that means a lot to me, Alena." Sue replied.

"Well, should we get going, or we might miss the best dresses to shine in." Alena said.

Sue smiled and agreed to go to the mall with Alena. She had planned to wear the dress ever to that dance with the best-looking guy in the whole school and make the girls all jealous of her for at least one night, because she was tired of being an outcast, because she was different. Both girls wanted to stand out at the dance, so they went from store to store, until they went into the most wonderful dress store, they had ever seen. It was from top to bottom with dresses of all shape, sizes, colors, and style.

Alena sense there was something off about the dress store.

"Sue, let us go somewhere else to shop for dresses." Alena asked.

"What, is wrong with this place, it has all kinds of dresses, and the dress I'm looking for might be in there." Sue said.

"Fine, let us make it quick; please Sue." Alena asked.

As the girls walk into Color Style: A Dress for All You Need, Sue started to look around to see what kind of dress she wanted, and the sales lady came over to her.

"Is there anything I can do for you young lady?" Sales Lady said.

"Yes, I want to try on that Gold Dress with the V-Neckline with lace going up the back, and a spilt going up the front of the right leg please." Sue asked.

"What can I get for young lady?" Sale lady asked Alena.

"No, thank you, just for my friend. I will find the dress I want at a different dress shop." Alena answered.

"Okay." Sales Lady said.

Sue went into the changing room, and Alena had notice that there was someone else there, when Alena went to take better look at the person, she discovered that all the girls who tried on dresses was out cold.

"Oh, no. Sue don't put the dress on it is very dangerous." Alena yelled.

It was too late she had the dress on, and it did look good on Sue, and her thin body, compared to Alena's average body. Then, Sue had begun to feel dizzy, and then she fell to the ground unconscious.

"What is going on?" Alena demeaned.

"So, you are one of those so-called guardians that has been giving us so much trouble. I have heard about that but for Morgana happened to be one of the best hutch men the Dark Kingdom Zodiac has." The sales lady said.

"Which guardian are you." The Sales Lady said.

"Which one are you? Why have you bother to show your ugly face in our presents here." Alena asked.

"The Dark Kingdom Zodiac, called me Poison Ivy. I happen to be one of the best but not as great as Morgana." Poison Ivy said.

"You think by playing with girls' emotions too look pretty for a special guy on their very first date is fun?" Alena said.

"I love the fact you think this is fun for me, but all I want to do is please my Dark Queen and Dark King, and by doing so I have to get rid of you." Poison Ivy said.

"Then bring it on. You mess with my best friend; you have made a grave mistake if you think I am just going to let you walk all over me. I am the guardian of the Crystal Star of water and ice. I am Alena, guardian of the Crystal Star of water and ice." Alena said.

"Water, I call you to me." Alena yelled.

"Your, water has no chance against me." Poison Ivy said.

"Dark power of the Dark Kingdom Zodiac come to me." Poison Ivy yelled.

"Vines, wrap her up, and take her life." Poison Ivy said.

"Poison Flowers bloom and fill this place with

poison. May these humans become part of the Dark Kingdom Zodiac as slaves to build our world, were the Majestic Star Kingdom will never rise." Poison Ivy said.

"Water Wall, protect the girls from the poison." Alena yelled.

Chapter 3

"You can't beat me with that weak waterpower you have guardian." Poison Ivy said.

"I will stop you even if you have me wrap up in this vine." Alena said.

"You can do it, guardian of the Crystal Star of ice and water." Mystery guy said.

"It is you again, can you help me?" Alena said.

"I will always help you, guardian as long as you keep up the good work you are doing and wanting to protect those you love the most." Mystery guy said.

"Fire come to me; burn the vines on the guardian." Mystery guy said.

"Thank you." Alena said.

"Now guardian; freeze these flowers and get rid of them." Mystery guy said.

"Ice come to me." Alena yelled.

"Please freeze these flowers to save all the girls." Alena said

As the flowers began to freeze so did Poison Ivy. She could not take the cold and so she disappeared.

Then before she knew it there was a cool wind to blow all the poison away from the people thanks to the Mystery guy in black coat, mask, and black plants. Alena had notice that his eyes stand out against the mask, they were a green color, and she felt that she had seen before. Before the Mystery guy could disappear again.

"Will she return just like Morgana?" Alena asked.

"She was one of the weaker droids of the Dark Kingdom Zodiac, so she will not have the power to return." Mystery guy said.

"Can you tell me who you are?" Alena asked.

"You can call me Knight Walker." Knight Walker said.

"Thank you again for the help." Alena said.

Alena went and checked on Sue, and the other girls to make sure they were okay. As she was walking to them the dress shop started to disappear because it was an illusion to hide the storage room. The dresses on the other hand stayed that were on the girls. The dresses were from a fine dress shop called Fantasy World: Then and Now. She made certain that the girls were okay, and then asked if they might have remembered how they got in the storage room, they all could not remember anything, except Sue, who had a very vague memory of what had happened.

"Sue, are you okay?" Alena asked

"Yes." Sue answered.

"Do you remember what happened?" Alena asked.

"Not, much but someone talking, and this guy that seemed so mysteries." Sue answered back.

"Okay, now that you have your dress, and paid for it let us go home okay." Alena said.

"Okay, but you have not got your dress yet for the dance that is coming next weekend." Sue said.

"That is okay; I will come back this weekend and get one." Alena answered Sue.

So, the girls left the storage room, still trying to remember how they got in there. Still cannot remember they just went on home and had forgotten all about what happened. Except for Sue who was trying to remember more about the last few hours and kept asking Alena who was that guy, and what happened, Alena kept avoiding the question, and did not want to answer Sue at this moment in time.

The next day, Sue was acting off, as if she were trying to remember a dream she might have had. Then next to her was Leroy talking to a boy I have never met before. I was wondering if he might be a new transfer student like Leroy was.

"Hi, Sue, Leroy, and new guy that I have never met before." Alena said.

"Hi." Sue and Leroy said together.

"This is my cousin from Italy. Joseph Ryan." Sue said.

"I never knew you had a cousin in a different country Sue." Alena said.

"Yeah, I'm sorry Alena, I had not seen him sense we have been very young, and before I met you." Sue said.

"Well, Joseph Ryan, how do you do." Alena said.

"Hi, Alena, Sue has been telling me a lot of things about you." Joseph said.

"What she did not tell me was how beautiful you are, with your raven color hair that goes down to your waist, light brown eyes, and tan skin tone. Please call me Joey." Joseph said.

"Thank you very much, I wish I could say the same about you, but Sue has never really told me anything about her family except her parents and younger brother, that I have met before. I am sorry I wish I could have more to say about that." Alena said.

As the four was talking, Alena could not help to think that Joey was not bad looking, he was not in the lead as Leroy, but in his own way he was quite good looking. With his light brown hair, hazel eyes, and his skin tone is a tan color. The four teenagers start to talk about school, and other teenage things. Alena started thinking about asking, Sue's cousin out on a date, because she is so tired of being shy and teased about it.

"Joey, I know this is short and we just met, would you like to see a movie with me someday soon?" Alena asked.

"Alena, I would love to see a movie with you any time, how about this weekend?" Joey said.

"That would be great sense I'm off work, this weekend, and I don't think my mother would mind." Alena said.

"Then, I will see you around 8pm Saturday." Joey said.

"Yes, that will be fine." Alena said.

Sue, and Leroy's mouth both dropped, they could not believe Alena would do that. Leroy was not happy with the fact that she wanted to go out with a guy she just met, instead of him. Sue could not believe she was not being shy like she usually is. Most of all; with her cousin, which he was so happy about this. As they started to talk about what movie they all want to see together, because Leroy was not going to let this boy come in and hit on the girl he truly wants to be with, he only went out with her best friend to make her very jealous, but it backed fired on him. So, he was not going to let her go off with this guy by herself.

"Why, don't we all go to the movies together?" Leroy said.

"I, agree with you." Sue said.

"Well, that is a good idea, that way we all can get to know each other better." Joey said.

"I'm okay with that." Alena said.

As they talked about what movie they wanted to see together, the bell had rung for the first period to start. As they are all walking to their homeroom, Joey started too spilt up from them.

"Joey, where is your homeroom at?" Sue asked.

"My homeroom is Math class." Joey said.

"Well see you later then Joey." Alena said.

"I have Science for my last class of the day." Joey said.

"I do to Joey. Let us be lab partners because I still do not have one since the beginning of school." Alena said.

"Yeah, well I do too." Leroy said.

"Then why don't you join our lab team and see if we can get along for Sue's sack." Alena suggested.

"I think that we can try to do that." Leroy said.

"It looks like we will become good friends and even better lab partners." Joey said. But Joey got the feeling that Leroy did not like him much. He was not for certain why but had a good thought to why. He was not happy with the fact that Alena had asked him out instead of Leroy which would make no sense at all because Leroy was with Sue.

Well as they spilt up to go to their homerooms, Alena was happy with herself because for once she did not what for the boy talk to her but her to talk to the boy. The three of them enter the English classroom to find that things were changed; Ms. Jones was splitting the class up into small groups to work on a project. Alena was hoping that Leroy would be in a different group than Sue and her. Do to her lack of good luck, the three of them was put into a group together which would make it hard as to the fact that the weekend was here, and they had to work on the project over the weekend which

"Isn't this your first date with Sue?" Joey asked Leroy.

"Yes, but we are all on a limited amount of money you know." Leroy said.

"Why, don't we eat at Hometown Buffet?" Alena suggested.

"Yeah, let's go there." Sue said.

"How are we going to afford a restaurant like that?" Leroy said.

"Simple, my mother is the owner and the Chef of the restaurant." Alena said.

"I agree." Sue said.

"So, it is settled then, let us meet there around 6:30pm." Alena said.

"FINE." Leroy, Joey, and Sue all said at the same time.

Well, they ate their lunch and then went back to class as for a Friday; they only do certain classes on Fridays. So, Alena, Sue, Leroy, and Joey went to Gym together. As they enter the gym room, they find out they are playing basketball for gym today. It was eight teams' groups of four to a team. So, they all agree to be on the same team, and for their first game against another group they won. Then it was time for the period to end, before they knew it, because they were having so much fun even through Alena was not that good when it came to sports, she did very well for someone who do not play sports very often. After class they all went to their next class, which met that Sue had math, and the rest had

made it hard for her to go out on her date w
She could not figure out why Sue and Leroy
to come with Joey and her to the movies in
place. As she knew Leroy hated her, he only p
to like her because of Sue. She just wanted t
know Joey better, because Sue never talks ab
family much.

Well, as the time went on in class the be
for lunch.

"Alena, come have lunch with us today, Jo
be eating with us too." Sue said.

"I agree with you Sue, she should have
with us." Leroy said.

"Okay Sue I will have lunch with you, but f
Leroy, why." Alena asked.

"Alena, you don't have to be like that." Sue

"The reason I agree is I think we should be
friends and get to know each other better for
Leroy answered.

"Fine." Alena replied.

Instead of going to the roof top like she al
did at this time each day of school, they went to
courtyard to meet up with Joey to have lunch
lunch went on, they were talking about what
should eat before the movies on Saturday n
at 8pm.

"We could have burgers and fries?" Le
suggested.

"No, it has to be better than that, buddy." Jo
said.

science to go to. As they enter their science room, they were cutting open frogs for the science lesson for the day and had to choose a partner to do the assignment with.

"Alena, would you like to be my partner for class today?" Joey asked.

"Sure!" Alena agreed.

Leroy was not happy about this and Joey stepping in on his future girlfriend or wife. He ended up being partners with another girl which had asked him out on date and to the dance next weekend, when he had turned her down, but that did not seem to matter to her. As the class and lesson went on Leroy kept watching Joey and Alena. He could not see what she saw in him, Joey was not bad looking, but compared to Leroy he was an average guy at best in his eyes. Well, the time had few by and it was at the end of class and school.

Today, Leroy, Sue, Alena, and Joey had walked home together talking about Saturday, and still not sure what movie too see, if it should be a romance, action, horror, and so on. So, they all agreed to call the movie theater to see what was playing the next day. Sue had called her mother to see if she could stay the night with Alena, and Alena had asked her mom if it would be okay for Sue to stay with her. Both parents agreed to the girls staying with each other, because they wanted to go shopping for an outfit for the movies and Alena wanted to get her dress for the dance that was next weekend.

So, the girls stayed up talking for many hours though the night and fell asleep at the same time. Well, they had asked Alena's mother to wake them around 10am in the morning so they can get a good start in their shopping for their new outfits, and Alena's new dress for the dance. The girls went to sleep; both were having a strange dream they could not make out. Alena has had the same dream before for the past month, but Sue just started to have these dreams just recently. Around the same time when Leroy had showed up, and even more now that her cousin was here. As the girl's dream, they were walking in the most beautiful palace; it was a place, with beautiful fields of flowers, as far as the eyes could see and some.

Sue was dreaming the same dream, but she was the center of attention by just one guy, in a gown that flowed to the floor in silver and gold term, lace going up her back with gems in the colors of the sun, and white as the moon. She was walking next to someone. When she looked to see who it was, she could not make out the face of the person, but knew she never wanted to leave his side. As they walked along, they enter the ballroom, and she started to look around to see who everyone was waiting for, then before she knew entered, Alena entered in the most beautiful dress she had seen on her. Her hair was as dark as a raven's feather down to her waist, light brown eyes, and the guy waiting for her was just as handsome as the tuxedo he was wearing. Alena was smiling from ear to ear.

><-><-O-<>-><

Alena was wearing this most beautiful dress she as ever seen; it was light blue, with sapphire crystals all over it, and a lace open back. It flowed to the floor and every turn she would sparkle. She was going some ware very special it seemed. She had entered a ballroom where there were people dancing, music playing, and in the middle of the floor was a guy wearing a sapphire tuxedo, with light blue crystals forming the collar, waiting for someone, and when she had entered the middle of the floor, the guy held out his hand to her.

"Will, you do me the honor of dancing with me." He asked.

"Yes, I would be honored to dance with you. Who are you? Why do you feel so familiar to me?" She said.

Alena could not help but blush when the guy took her hand, and they started to dance. All the eyes in the ballroom were on them and following their every move. She could not help but keep smiling because it was so romantic, that if she would wake, because she knew she was dreaming, she would never get the dream back. She felt so happy as if he and she were met for each. It was as if they have been here before and had done this more than once. She felt as if she was met to be here, as if she had finally found her place in the world. Then as the alarm was going off someone was shaking her and here it was her mother waking the girls to get up so they could get started on their shopping before their date tonight.

"Sue and Alena, get up." Alena's mother said.

"Were up mom, please stop shaking me." Alena asked.

"I am, up Ms. Patches. Thank you." Sue said halfway a wake.

As the girls are getting dress, Alena was thinking about the dream she just had, and could not hope that someday this guy would be real for her to really touch. Be the dream of a lifetime. Sue was thinking about the dream too, she could not hope that someday soon she would get to meet that mystery person walking next to her. She was so happy with the gown she was wearing that the one she had gotten at the mall the other day when Alena and she went could not even add up to the dress in her dream. Alena wanted to ask Sue about the dream and if she might have had one.

"Sue, by any chance did you have an odd dream last night?" Alena asked.

"Yes, What about you Alena?" Sue asked her.

"Yes, I did, it was about a ballroom, people dancing, music playing, and this really cute guy." Alena replied

"Same for me, I was wearing this most beautiful gown that flowed all the way down to the floor in the colors of silver and gold, with termed in gems of gold and silver, like the sun and moon." Sue said.

"The dress I was wearing was a light blue, with sapphire crystals going up it all over, with an open back." Alena said.

"That sounds beautiful Alena." Sue said.

"So does yours, Sue." Alena said.

As the girls kept talking about the dream, they each had, they were finally dress and heading to the mall for a little shopping before their date with the guys tonight. It was 11 am by the time they had left the house for the mall.

As the girls enter the mall, they ran into someone, because they were too busy talking about the dreams that they were not watching were they were going.

"We are so sorry." Sue and Alena said together.

"It is okay girls." The women said.

When Alena seen who it was, she could not believe her eyes.

"Jennifer, we are so sorry." Alena said.

"Ah, Alena it is nice to see you again, it is quite alright." Jennifer said.

"Who, is you lovely friend, Alena." Jennifer asked.

"Sue this is Jennifer Muse, Jennifer this is my best friend, Sue Stang." Alena replied.

"It is nice to meet you, Sue Stang." Jennifer said.

"It is nice to meet you as well, Jennifer Muse." Sue said.

"Well, take care girls." Jennifer said.

"You are too." Alena and Sue said together.

"How do you know her, Alena?" Sue asked.

"She started to work at my mom's restaurant the other day as a new cook." Alena answered Sue.

As the girls went on, they started to look for outfits for the date tonight. Sue had found this very nice mini skirt, with a red top, and flat shoes since Sue was thin and tall. Alena had found a nice pair of black skinny pants, with a baby doll top that was pink, some heels so that she looked a little taller than what she was. The girls finally went to a dress shop to find Alena a nice dress for the dance. The girls entered Star World, where all the famous actors go to get nice dresses for the Grammys. As the girls enter Alena notice this most beautiful dress that was pink with light blue trim, open lace back, with blue shimmer in the fabric. As the girls buy the dress. They went to Shoe World to find the best heels to go with the dresses they got. Sue has gotten a pair of heels that were gold and silver gems that laced up her legs, like ballet slippers. Alena had gotten a pair of light blue heels, with pink crystals on the toes, and a strap going across her ankle. As the girls finished their shopping; they notice they had an hour to get ready before meeting the boys at the restaurant, then going to the movies.

Chapter 4

As the girls are getting ready for the night with the boys. Alena starts to get the feeling something is not right. Well, the girls left the house to meet the guys at the restaurant. As they walk down to the restaurant, which was not that far from the house, the girls looked very nice. As they walk up to the guys which were stunned by their beauty. As the four friends go into the restaurant to have dinner, they choose what type of movie they all wanted to see. They all choose to go to a horror movie because the girls did not want romance right now.

As they go to the movies, they enter the theater and something was off, but the friends went into the movie. As they are watching the movie something was going on, everyone was getting tired. As Alena looks on her friends start to fall asleep during the movie. Alena could not understand why. Then it hit her that feeling she was having this morning, and throughout the day.

"What is going on here?" Alena asked.

"Ah, so tell me guardian, what does life mean to you?" Mystery person said.

"What do you mean?" Alena said.

"How do you feel about life?" Mystery person said.

"Life means, a lot to me, it is special, it has ups and downs." Alena said.

"I will take your life then. As well as the soul that is as pure as the moon at night." Mystery person said.

"So let me guess you are from the Dark Kingdom Zodiac. So which general are you?" Alena asked.

"Blair, I will take your life, these humans' lives, they will serve our Dark Kingdom whether it be willing, or by force." Blair said.

"So you are after souls, humans, just so they will serve your Dark Kingdom?" Alena said.

"Yes, I will start with you, and your friends." Blair said.

"I will not let you, destroy life." Alena said.

"Dark Power; come to me." Blair said.

"Water; come to me. Protect us and everyone here." Alena said.

"You can't stop me; with my powers they are stronger than those you have come against before." Blair said.

"Darkness, take away her sight." Blair said.

"Water walls protect those I care about." Alena said.

"Guardian of The Crystal Star of water and ice, let us combine our powers again." Knight Walker.

"Yes, let us combine our powers to bet this enemy." Alena said.

"Wind; come to me." Knight Walker said.

"Water; come to me." Alena said.

"Water Vortex!" Alena and Knight Walker said together.

When the enemy is defeated, everyone started to wake up. She had to go before anyone could notice her. As time passed by, she ended up missing the entire movie and had to call Sue, Leroy, and Joey to say she was sorry, because she told them she was sick that is why she left the movies.

As it is she could not remember much over the weekend because of what happened Saturday, she was not sure if her friends will every talk to her again because of what had happened. So, for Sunday she worked at the restaurant the whole day. To her luck Joey came in to see her.

"Hi, Alena." Joey said.

"Hi." Alena said.

"I am sorry about last night. I was not feeling very well. It was something I might have eaten before the movie." Alena said.

"It is okay. How are you feeling today?" Joey said.

"A lot better, then what I was feeling last night." Alena said.

"I'm glad, then maybe we can have a dinner another time just the two of us?" Joey asked.

"I would really like that." Alena answered.

Then as they were talking, Joey; lend in and kissed Alena for the first time. She blushed and her face turned very red. As she looked up Leroy was standing in the doorway with a dozen roses for her. She could not understand why he looked so mad; he was with her best friend.

"I see you are feeling better Alena. These flowers are from Sue and me." Leroy said.

"Thank you, please tell Sue I'm feeling better today it was only the stomach flu." Alena said.

"I'm sorry if I might have interrupted you two." Leroy said.

As he was walking out the restaurant, he sat the roses on the nearest table and walked out and seemed to be very upset.

"What was his problem?" Joey said.

"I'm not sure, he seemed upset." Alena said.

"I don't see why he would be upset, when he is with my cousin." Joey said.

"He seemed to be hurt." Alena said.

"Why, because I kissed my girlfriend." Joey said.

"When did we become girlfriend and boyfriend Joey?" Alena said.

As she was saying this, she was smiling from ear to ear about the thought of being his girlfriend.

"We became girlfriend and boyfriend, just now." Joey said.

As he was saying this he was smiling from ear to ear because he felt that he had the most beautiful girlfriend in the whole world, and most of all he had the most beautiful girl in the whole school. So, for the rest of the day Joey had helped at the restaurant, just so he could be close to Alena. He did not understand why he needed to be close to her, but something tells him he needs to protect her from something.

As the day had come to an end, Joey walked Alena home in a moon light walk. Which in Alena's eyes was very romantic; so, she took it all in. Joey had kisses her again, this time to say goodbye, and good night.

As Joey is leaving, Alena loves the thought that Joey was being romantic and all, but something seemed off, as if this were not right. She loves that she had a boyfriend for once in her life.

Chapter 5

Alena woke the next day happy about going to school, and she got dress in a hurry. As she is walking to school, she could not help but think about the kiss she got from Joey yesterday. Then as she was thinking Leroy's face popped into her mind and the hurt that was on his face when he saw that Joey had kissed her. What she did not get was why he was upset about it. It was like he did not want her to be happy, or even to have a boyfriend, it was as if he was very jealous of Joey. Was he happy with Sue? Alena was thinking. If not, then why did he agree to go to the dance with her, and out on a date with her Saturday? As Alena walks to school, she wonders if Leroy might like her, then it hit her. He likes her in so many ways that she did not notice, but he is with her best friend, and she is with Joey, they just started to go out. So, she is going to find out why Leroy was so upset yesterday when he came to the restaurant.

As she walks into the courtyard, she meets up with Joey, and they walk to the big Oak Tree that they meet at where Sue, and Leroy where standing. As they start to walk up to the tree Leroy bends in and kisses Sue right in front of her. She felt as if the world had stopped spinning. She did not know why she would feel like this when she is with Joey.

"WOW, you two!" Joey said.

"Yeah, wow!" Alena said.

Leroy started to smile because of the look on Alena's face, when she saw him kiss her best friend. Joey was laughing because it was funny that Leroy would do this to make Alena and him jealous. It was so bad that he would go this far while they are at school. The bell rang for first period, so the friends walked to their first periods. As Alena, Sue, and Leroy walk to the back of the classroom to sit. The girls started to talk about what had happened.

"Sue, what was the kiss like? Did it make your leg pop?" Alena asked.

"It was magical. Yes, my leg did pop some." Sue replied.

"Have you kissed Joey yet? I mean not that I want to know because he is my cousin." Sue asked.

"I do not kiss and tell, but yes it was different. Not what I was excepting, but great either way." Alena replied.

"What do you mean?" Sue asked.

"It was really nice and romantic." Alena said.

"Why, does it matter to you?" Leroy said.

"Well, I was just making sure that Sue enjoyed it." Alena replied.

"What you think that I'm not a good kisser, and how would you know?" Leroy said.

"I would not know. I do not want to know either; you are with my best friend." Alena said.

"That is enough you two!" Sue said.

"I agree. If you two keep it up, you will go stay in the hall together." Ms. Jones said.

As they kept arguing back and forth Ms. Jones kicked them out of class.

"You two can go stand in the hallway until the period is over and you both go to lunch." Ms. Jones said.

As the two of them walk into the hall, they are still talking about what happened in the courtyard just before class.

"What is your problem?" Alena asked.

"I don't have the problem." Leroy replied.

"There is something wrong because you are more of a jerk then you were the first time, I met you." Alena said.

"Let's talk about you, then." Leroy replied.

"What about me?" Alena asked.

"Well, when you first saw me, you kept staring at me as if you were undressing me with your eyes." Leroy said.

"You are so full of yourself. I was not undressing you with my eyes." Alena said.

"Then explain to me why you kept staring the first day I started school here. On another note, what do you see in Joey?" Leroy asked.

"I thought I, might have met you before. What is going with me, and Joey is none of your damn business." Alena said.

"Whatever; you say." Leroy said.

As they are standing in the hallway, they become a little uneasy. Like something seemed to be wrong. Then before Alena and Leroy knew it something strange happened. Before Alena knew she was being knocked down by Leroy. When she looked up a plasma ball hit him; the plasma ball had been aimed at Alena, and he protected her. But why would he protect her, they hate each other.

"Are you okay?" Leroy said.

"Why would you protect me?" Alena asked.

"I do not know I just moved. I did not think about it. Are you okay?" Leroy said.

"Yes, as Alena started to cry." Alena replied.

"Why are you crying?" Leroy asked.

"I don't know why, you got hurt because of me." Alena replied.

"Please do not cry. You have a big heart, Alena." Leroy said.

As they were sitting there Alena could not believe that the Dark Kingdom Zodiac would attack her at school. As she is sitting Leroy had passed out from being hit by the plasma ball.

"Who are you?" Alena demanded.

"I will not tell you guardian, if you can find me then I will reveal myself to you." Mystery person said.

"Then where are you?" Alena asked.

"Follow by voice, and you will find me, but if you are to late your friends, classmates, and everyone here will be under my spell, and give themselves to the Dark Kingdom Zodiac." Mystery person said.

Alena followed the voice like requested. As she is following the voice she notices where she was heading. It was the cafeteria and as she went through the doors, she notices that the students that were having lunch passed out because of the spell.

"I am here. Who are you?" Alena said.

"I'm the general of fire." Mystery person said.

"So do you plain on using dark fire to stop me." Alena said.

"Ah, that would be so much fun to do, but with your water and ice powers my dark fire power does not stand a chance against that. So, I Victoria will use it on your friends and this lame school of yours." Victoria said.

"Victoria, you are going to use dark fire to hurt these people." Alena asked.

"NO!! I am going to use dark fire to kill them." Victoria said.

"Well go luck with that." Mystery guy said.

"Who are you?" Alena and Victoria said together.

"I am the guardian of summoning. My Star Crystal is the Summoning Star." Mystery guy said.

"What is your name?" Alena asked.

"My beautiful raven hair beauty, I'm Joseph Ryan." Joey said.

"How is this even possible? Your, Sue's cousin." Alena asked.

"Yes. I am. I am also one of the twelve guardians like you." Joey said.

"Alena let us finish this evil and save our friends, and students at this school." Joey said.

"I'm with you." Alena said.

"I summon the dragon of Water." Joey yelled.

"I call ice to me." Alena said.

"Ice storm rain down on her dark fire and save these people that we care about." Alena and Joey yelled together.

Chapter 6

"Dark Flame destroy everything in sight. Leave nothing untouched. We are going to take this as a Dark Zodiac Kingdom spot to enforce our powers." Victoria yelled.

Alena was watching she could not help but, be thankful for the help that Joey was giving. As the dark flames tried to engulf everything the ice stormed had stopped it. There was a frozen flame in the middle of the cafeteria and ice rain was coming down, and with a dragon flying overhead.

"Water; come to me. I will not let you destroy this place and make it a place of evil power." Alena said.

As she uses the water to help clean up the dark flames for which Victoria had called, she realized that she could still be somewhere in the school. But as the flames cleaned, she saw someone turned to ash, as she was looking Joey was coming over to her.

"You did well guardian of the Crystal Star of water and ice." Joey said.

"You did well too, guardian of the Crystal Star of Summing." Alena said.

Then Joey bent down and kisses her, she was happy for the help and very grateful that he came because the other one did not. She was happy that they could save their friends and the whole school. At last, she had someone to talk to about being one of the twelve guardians of the Majestic Star Kingdom.

"Joey, do you know anything about being a guardian?" Alena asked.

"Yes, I have been a guardian for a long time." Joey said.

"Do, you know a Jennifer Muse?" Alena asked.

"Ah one of two protectors, yes, I know who she is. She and another came and found me when I was 12 years old." Joey said.

"I'm surprised that it took them so long to find you." Joey said.

"I do not think I am the only guardian they have found here. There is this guy he calls himself the Knight Walker, and I think Sue, might be a guardian too, because she was born with a few gifts as was I." Alena said.

"It would not surprise me if she were one." Joey said.

As the two friends kept talking about the guardians and what had happened today. The students had started to wake and before they knew it school was over. The fight must have taken longer than before, as Joey and Alena were walking to the courtyard to meet up with Leroy and Sue, the only one they seen was Sue at the big oak tree.

"Sue, I thought Leroy would be here with you?" Alena and Joey asked.

"He was, but he felt sick and wanted to go straight home, but he would not tell me what was wrong with him." Sue replied.

"I'm sorry Sue; I think that might have been my fault, because we had gotten into it in the hallway after Mrs. Jones kicked us out of class." Alena said with a sad face.

"I will check on him later." Sue said.

"Why, don't we all check on him later, because he is our friend too." Joey said.

"I agree." Sue and Alena said together.

Then Sue started to smile and was happy that her favorite cousin was here to help. As the three friends start walking home, they run into none other than Jennifer Muse.

"Hi Jenny." Alena said.

"Hi Alena, Sue, and Joey." Jennifer said.

"How do you know Joey?" Sue asked.

"I meet Mr. Ryan a long time ago at school. I was a sub for his teacher." Jennifer said.

"Oh, okay." Sue said.

"Alena I was wondering if we can start your training today?" Jennifer said.

"I think that would be a good idea." Joey said.

"Okay, Sue I will go with you over to Leroy's

house later, okay. Joey, would you like to come over and help with my training?" Alena replied.

"That would be great." Jennifer said.

"I would love too. Sue, you do not mind if I spend time together with Alena this afternoon, and meet up with you later to go over to Leroy's?" Joey said.

"No, I don't mind; just call me you two when you are done with training, okay." Sue said.

"Okay." Alena and Joey said together.

As the three friends spilt up, Sue went on home as for Joey and Alena they headed to a warehouse to start training. As they are walking up to the warehouse, Alena was thinking that this could be a good think for her and Joey because now they have something in common than just looks.

"Is this being we are going to train for now on?" Alena asked.

"Yes." Jennifer said.

"Are you happy that I am a guardian, Alena?" Joey asked.

"Yeah, I am because then I won't be alone in defending the new Majestic Star Kingdom." Alena had replied.

As the three walks into the warehouse to start training, Alena still had million questions for both Jenny and Joey. She let the questions to flow from her mind so that she was able to focus on the task at hand, and that was learning to control her powers a lot better than what she does. As they walk into the warehouse, they notice there is a lot of ropes, chains, platforms, and many other things that Alena could not put a name now. So, they go into the warehouse to start training.

"So where do we start." Alena asked.

"You my dear, will start with calling water to you." Jennifer said.

"Joey, you can summon the dragon of ice." Jennifer said.

"Water; come to me." Alena said.

"I summon you, Ice Dragon come to me." Joey said.

"Now, that you two have called your abilities to you. Combined your powers together make a new attack." Jennifer said.

"Ice Strom" Joey and Alena yelled together.

"Good, now try something different." Jennifer said.

"Water; come to me." Alena said.

"I summon you, Wind Dragon come to me." Joey said.

"Water Vortex" Alena and Joey yelled together.

"That is great; I see you two have learned to use your powers. When you two can master your skills, you will be great. Keep up the good work; we will train daily if it is possible." Jennifer said.

"Thank you." Alena and Joey said together.

As they had kept training into the night, Joey walked Alena home to make sure she was okay after the day they have had. It was a cool night a chance of snow, and it was peaceful. As they walked, they talked about how to check on Leroy and Sue, as well as why Leroy would get upset about them being together. So, when they got to Alena's house Joey wanted no more than anything to kiss her on this peaceful night. So, he lends into her, and they kissed each other for a good long time. When the kiss ended with Joey being breathless, but Alena loved the kiss, but it was not the breath taking away kind that is only in fairy tales, for which she longed.

Alena went into her house to get ready for dinner and bed, she was walking into the diner room she smelled the most delicious food she has every smelled from her mom's cooking. As she walks into the diner room, she sees none other than Leroy Addams sitting at the table waiting to eat.

"What are you doing here?" Alena asked.

"I came to let you know that I was okay, after yesterday and that it was just a shock to see him kiss you." Leroy said.

"Oh, thanks and glad that you are okay." Alena said.

As she sat down at the table to get ready to eat dinner, Leroy lends in and reminder her that they had a project to do because it was already late. So, they asked for them to turn it in late which must be done by Friday.

"What did you and Joey do today?" Leroy asked.

"We spent time together, and it is none of your business." Alena answered.

"Yeah, well I don't trust him." Leroy replied.

"Since when did you care about me and who I go out with?" Alena said.

"I have always cared about you; you just choose not to see it." Leroy said.

"What, you are with my best friend. What about Sue?" Alena asked.

"You miss understand, I care about you as a friend. I care about Sue very much." Leroy said.

"Whatever, you say." Alena said.

"We will let us meet with Sue to do our project tomorrow okay. Around 4pm Tuesday after school." Leroy said.

"Fine" Alena said.

"Fine, then I will see Sue and you tomorrow after school." Leroy said.

"Have you talked to Sue about this?" Alena asked.

"Yes, she is okay with the time. You can call her to make sure." Leroy replied.

As time went on, they said good night after dinner. Alena went up to her room to finish her homework from the day; she started to think about why Leroy would be so concern about her love life. As she is sitting in her room with the twin bed, posters; of all kinds of famous people, her favorite band, pink wallpaper, and pictures her mother has put into her room of her when she was younger, and family pictures. She could not stop thinking about what Leroy had said to her tonight. He was really concerned about her. What she did not know was why, he would be so concerned with what she does, and who she might be with; most of all he was really bent over her spending time with Joey. As she sat thinking forgetting about her homework, but something was still bugging her about why Leroy would be upset, at her house at night, even more cold than usually. Was Leroy that bent out of shape about her and Joey? Alena was thinking.

As she sat in her room she got up and moved to the window to look at the stars, because it always claimed her and cleared her mind. As she was looking at the stars, she notices that the night was very bright, and the stars was shining well. As she went to her bed she dozed off into an uneasy sleep. She kept having this bad dream that would come and go. Sometimes it was nice, and sometimes it could be bad.

Alena was dreaming that an evil had attacked this beautiful kingdom that looked like it shined for many years. The evil was so bad that it would overtake the minds of the people that lived there, their bodies, their spirits, and their lives. As she saw what was happening to her people, she wanted to save them as she did, she saw the most beautiful woman ever, as the women walked into her room she started to speak to Alena.

"Hi my dear." The Queen said.

"Hi, mom." Alena said.

"I see you are not happy with how things are." The Queen said.

"Yeah, why does this Dark Kingdom want to destroy the peace we have here?" Alena said.

"I am not sure, but your father and I will keep fighting to keep that peace. I need you to be very strong because one day we may not be able to stop this evil." The Queen said.

"I will do what is expected of me." Alena said.

"That is great my dearest daughter." The Queen said.

"I love you very much mom." Alena said.

"Ah, I beg to dipper. There is someone you love even more than your father, me, and this kingdom, for which you would give your life for." The Queen said.

"Yes, he is very special. He comes from this far off galaxy that is very peaceful, beautiful, and has the most wonderful life there is." Alena said.

Chapter 7

As Alena was dreaming, she could not help wondering if this might have been a past life. As she had waked the next day she kept thinking about the dream, unlike the others she remembered everything about this dream than she could about the others. Who was this guy she was so head over heels about because she could not stop thinking about him or the Queen? Who was the Queen, what was she like, did she love her or was this all-Alena imagination going crazy. Why do these dreams keep coming when she sleeps, and they have gotten worse since Leroy showed up? When she has a disagreement with Leroy, she has the darkest dreams she has ever had. Again, why does this keep happening to her?

As she was wondering her mother yells up the stairs.

"Alena time for school." Alena's mom yelled.

"Mom, I am not feeling good today. Can I stay home from school?" Alena yelled back.

"What is wrong dear?" Alena's mom asked.

"My stomach is very upset; I can't keep anything down." Alena told her mother.

"It sounds like you might have the stomach flu." Alena's mom said.

Leroy was very good looking; he is at least five'11 and the darkest black hair she has ever seen on a guy, eyes as dark as the forest, skin as dark as a Native American she has read about in history books, very strong and cares. For her she is average in her own mind. With hair as dark as a raven's feather, clear down past her butt, skin color of a light tan color, her eyes were a light brown to honey color, with a little hint of green, and she stands five'2. As she looked at herself in the mirror, she could not see what both Joey and Leroy seen in her. Joey was six'2, Hazel eyes, light brown hair, not as tan as her or Leroy, but not white like a ghost. Sue was very pretty she stands five'8, blue eyes, blonde hair as yellow as the sun, skin color a dark tan, but she did not know why she was feeling this way. Why was she comparing herself to Sue, Leroy, and Joey, did she not belong in the same group as they did. So, as she was looking at herself in the mirror, she notices that these two guys were not the only guys that would check her out at school. What she did not want was a guy who was after her body. After her soul that can make the world stand still, take her breath away with just one look, and a kiss she never wants to stop. These are all pipe dreams, and the dream she had last night shows there is a guy that is right for her. She really likes Joey, but he does not seem to be the right guy. Yes, she was secretly crushing on Leroy, since the first day she met him at school. She does not want to hurt Sue, she is her best friend. What, Alena did not know was why does everything have to be so complicated, what is it she really wants. She is a guardian, she can control water and ice, and she is pretty in her own way, what has her so confused.

As Alena was still thinking about all that was going on around her, she also wondering if any her friends or boyfriend would miss her at school today?

>─┤─◆>─O─<◆>┤─<

As Sue walks to school, she gets a call on her cell phone; it was Alena calling to tell her she would not be at school today because she was sick. As she was walking, she runs into someone.

"I'm so sorry mister." Sue said.

"It is alright my dear." The guy said.

"Where are you going with such a sad face my dear?" Guy asked.

"Well, I am heading to school, the reason I seem so sad today is that my best friend is sick." Sue said.

"Oh, I am sorry to hear that." Guy said.

"What is your name?" Guy said.

"Oh, I am so sorry. My name is Sue Stang." Sue replied.

"Well Sue it is nice to meet you. My name is Andrew. You can call me Andy." Andy said.

Andy was a tall mocha looking guy with eyes as dark as the earth, hair as light as a cloud. He was a good-looking guy in Sue's eyes, but he was older than her.

"It was nice meeting you to Andy." Sue said.

Sue kept walking to school she runs into Joey and Leroy on the school grounds.

"Hi Leroy, and Joey." Sue said.

"Hi." Leroy and Joey said together.

"What is up with you two?" Sue asked.

"Well, I get a call from my girlfriend telling me she will not be at school today because she is sick." Joey said.

"Alena called me too." Sue said.

"What does it matter, if she is here or not?" Leroy said.

"It does matter." Joey and Sue said together.

"Well, I think that she is just full of herself." Leroy said.

"Oh; really! So, if I might be mistaken did not you get upset the other day when I kissed her?" Joey said.

"That was just you seen things. Why would I get upset with you kissing her when I am with Sue, who is ten times better looking than Alena?" Leroy said.

"Hold on you two, first do not compare me to Alena, she is my best friend. Not only is that she pretty in her own way, just like me." Sue said.

"Sorry." Leroy said.

"Good then let us get to class. She will be feeling better later to meet us at the park to do our English assignment." Sue said to Leroy.

"Okay." Leroy said.

"See you later Sue." Joey said.

As the three friends spilt up to go to their homerooms. Joey was thinking about how Leroy reacted to Alena not being at school, and then getting very touchy when he mentioned the day, he had kissed Alena in the restaurant. What is his deal? Joey kept wondering. It is like he wants her but acts as if she does not matter. Well, he was not about to let Leroy get to him about his girlfriend. He was planning to call her after school, to see if she is doing better. As Joey kept thinking about Alena, her being guardian, this evil trying to take over everything, Jennifer, Leroy, Sue, and himself what is happening he was surprised that no one has noticed. He was thinking that those who have been attacked do not remember anything, and that they got their control back of them self. He could not stop wondering what will happen if this keeps up.

>—+—<>—O—<>—+—<

Sue walked into her homeroom with Leroy, as they always did, they walked back to the back of the classroom to sit. As she was sitting there, she could not help but keep looking over to where Alena usually sits next to her in class and Leroy on the other side of her. What she did not understand was why Leroy became so cold hearted about Alena, than he normally is.

"Leroy is there something going on between you and Alena?" Sue asked before class started.

"What would make you think that and say that?" Leroy replied.

"Well, you are a little colder than normal today when Alena is talked about or even seen?" Sue said.

"Well, I'm sorry I just realized that she was way different than I thought she was." Leroy said.

"What do you mean by that?" Sue asked as she is started to get angry.

"I mean that she turned out to be someone different than I wanted to get to know even better. She is not the same person I thought she might be." Leroy said.

Before Sue could say another word class started. As she sat there thinking about what is going on with Leroy and Alena, she could not help but feel a little jealousy of her best friend. She knew that Leroy was out of her league for being a boyfriend type, but he asked her out, but she still felt that he might have feelings for Alena and not her. That she was just there to sink his hook into. As she sat there in class hoping it would be over soon, because they only had a half day today, she could go over to Alena's house and find out what is going on. Well as she was sitting there, she started to think about

Andy the guy she met this morning on her way to school. He was most definitely good looking. She felt bad because she was with a good-looking guy, but he was into another person other than her. She knew Leroy liked Alena a lot, but she did not know why he would ask her out instead of Alena. She will eventually break it off with Leroy after the dance this coming weekend or a little way down the line.

>⊶⊷⊙⊶⊷⊰

Leroy sat next to Sue in class today and could not help but think about Alena instead of Sue. He could not believe Sue would ask him that kind of question most of all about her best friend. He was started to wonder if Sue was started to catch on to why he had asked her out in the first place. What bugged him most; was that Alena knew he had feelings for her but choose to go out with Joey. There was a connection between her and him that he could not ignore. He knows she felt it too. Yet he was with her best friend, and she was with her best friend's cousin. Most of all he was having this dream about a princess that he needed to find, and all he could do was keep thinking about Alena all day long. If he did not find the princess soon the whole world or more would go into craziness. He knew that if the dreams did not stop soon, he was going to go crazy without sleep. He wanted to be near Alena more than anything but knew that the person waiting for him may never be found. What he also did not understand was that he would black out at times and when he came too bad things had happened. What is going on with me? Leroy was thinking. Why does it matter if I find this girl or not. I need to find out who I am before I can help anyone out. What he did not tell his friends or classmates was that the guy who was his father had adopted him when he was a baby. He had a good life, and he was getting ready to turn sixteen soon. His father was looking at cars for him, if he kept his grades up and made friends. He did have great grades, he made a few friends, one that he is very jealousy of but still they are his friends. So, his father was looking at cars for his sixteen birthday which is in a few weeks. Not only does he have his birthday coming up; the dance is in a few days. He was taking Sue, while Joey was taking Alena. All he could do was deal with it and hope that sooner than later Joey and Alena breaks up, and Sue and he breaks up so that he could ask Alena out before another guy steps in.

As the two sit behind the classroom the bell rang for the day to end since they only had one exam today and the rest were the next day, Alena would have to make up the exam because she missed the day, but Sue was hoping she was feeling better, so that they can get their project done. So, they all can get full credit and have a good grade to finish the class with. As the two walk out of the school building Joey comes running up to them.

"Hey, is either of you two going to go check on Alena?" Joey asked.

"Yeah, I'm going." Sue said.

"Well can I come along I want to make sure she is okay to." Joey replied.

"That will be fine Joey she is your girlfriend. Leroy will you be coming along too?" Sue asked.

"No, I will meet you at the park to do our project. Please tell her I hope she feels better soon." Leroy said.

As Sue, Leroy, and Joey are walking, Sue's cell phone started to ring. "Hello?" Sue asked.

"Hey Sue, it is me Alena, I will meet you and Leroy at the park to do our project. Please tell everyone I am okay and that the stomach flu passed." Alena said.

"Okay, I will tell them." Sue said.

"Well, there is a change of plans Alena is going to meet us at the park to work on our project. She said to tell you both she was feeling a lot better. Joey why do not you come to the park to help us, and you can see Alena." Sue said.

"That would be great." Joey said.

The friends headed to the park. By the fountain was a girl sitting with raven dark hair. So, all three walked up to her to make sure it was Alena, as they approached her, she was reading something.

"Hey." Joey, Sue, and Leroy said together.

"Hey everyone." Alena said.

"Have you been waiting long?" Joey asked.

"No, I just got here a few minutes ago." Alena said.

"That is cool." Joey said.

"Thanks." Alena said.

"Where should we go to do our project? There are many places around here and on the school campus that we can pull up some grass and sit so that we can get started." Alena asked.

"Let us go over to the shelter house and do it. That way we can have some shade from the sun and stay cool because it is a very warm day." Leroy said.

"I agree." Sue said.

All four of them walked over to the shelter house to start their project, which was on poets from the 1800's. As they are walking up to sit down Leroy sat next to Sue and Joey sat next to Alena. The reason they choose the park was because it has been so warm lately, they wanted to sit outside and do their project and enjoy the nice weather they are having for it being the middle of winter. The temperature is 85 degrees and it made it very nice to be outside with all their friends.

"Has anyone done any research on poets of the 1800's?" Alena asked.

"I could not find any." Sue replied.

"That is okay. We can do it together." Alena said.

As they worked on their project something started to seem off to Alena. She could not understand why, she started to feel like this.

"Do you feel that?" Alena whispered to Joey.

"Yeah" Joey said.

They started to look around and notice that the people that were enjoying the day started to run and as they are running, they start too clasped from something. As they are started to get up to see what was going on and go check on the people Leroy and Sue started to fall asleep.

"Sue, Leroy, you need to get out of here." Alena and Joey yelled.

"What is going on?" Sue and Leroy said.

Before Alena and Joey could answer them, they had passed out. Alena was wondering who could do this and then it hit. It was the Dark Kingdom Zodiac.

"Who are you?" Alena and Joey asked together.

"Well, I see I have found to guardians." Odd person said.

"What do you want with us?" Alena asked.

"Well, my dream is to get rid of everyone with a good heart. Take over this place and turn all these mere humans into slaves for my Dark Queen and Dark King." Odd person said.

"So which general are you?" Joey asked.

"Ah, guardian wouldn't you like to know." Odd person said.

"Don't mock me." Joey said.

"Have you found your princess yet guardian of Summoning?" Odd person said.

"If I did your dark kingdom would not still be standing. You would not be here in this time and space." Joey said. As he is saying this the park around them started to die and the sky started to get dark.

"What do you mean? What princess are you talking about?" Alena asked.

"Hello guardian of water and ice you have not been told yet" Odd person said and started to lough.

"Well tell you later, Alena." Joey said.

"Fine, we need to get these people and our friends to a safe place." Alena said.

"I agree with you." Joey said.

"Not a chance." Odd person said.

As Alena and Joey try to get the people to a safe place the odd person put every person into a cage. Set black flames to it, to keep them from getting to the people. As they are trying to get the people freed Joey and Alena are put into a cage to keep them from getting away and saving the people that are trapped.

"What can we do Joey?" Alena asked.

"We fight with everything we got." Joey replied.

"I want to, but my powers are being drained." Alena said.

"Just hold on." Joey said.

As Joey is saying this, he felt his powers being drained along with Alena. He could not understand why this is happening. What are they going to do to stop this evil?

"I will take you both to by my Dark Queen and King." The Dark Phoenix said.

"I will help you out." Knight Walker said.

"Oh, and what are you going to do?" Dark Phoenix said.

"Water; come to me." Knight Walker yelled.

"Stop the dark flames on their cage." Knight Walker said.

As the water's healing powers stop the dark flames the cage breaks. Joey and Alena fall to the ground. Knight Walker caught Alena before she could hit the ground as Joey landed on his feet.

"Thank you, Knight Walker." Alena said.

"There is no time for that; thank you." Joey said.

Chapter 8

"Water Dragon; come to me." Joey summoned. As they all turn around to see that there are so many people that have been captured and put into cages on a very beautiful day in the park has turned into a nightmare for them.

"Free the people from those dark cages." Joey asked. When he is saying this the cages seem to start to shrink smaller causing some of the people to scream out in pain.

"Ice; come to me." Alena yelled. While the ice is forming it starts to freeze the cages and the people in them because there is a curse on the cages caused by the Dark Kingdom Zodiac fighter.

"Freeze the Dark Phoenix over." Alena yelled.

As their powers did what they wanted, the Dark Phoenix was toasted by the power of the Crystal Stars of Water and Ice and Summoning. The Dark Phoenix is no more. Then something happened that never happened before.

"You little guardians think you can bet us Dark Kingdom Zodiac." Dark King said.

"Who are you?" Alena, Joey, and Knight Walker said together.

"I'm the Dark King of the Dark Kingdom Zodiac." Dark King said.

"What do you want with these people?" They asked together.

"I need them to free us from this hell we were put into by the Queen and King of Majestic Star Kingdom. When I find the prince and princess of the Majestic Star Kingdom, I will tear them apart, and force the princess which is the rightful era to the throne of Majestic Star Kingdom to marry our Dark Prince of the Dark Kingdom Zodiac. He will rule for all eternally as the King of Majestic Star Kingdom. Not that so called prince of the Light Kingdom." Dark King said.

"We will stop you, some way and somehow." Alena said.

"Ah, you are quite the beauty guardian of the Crystal Star of water and ice." Dark King said.

"Leave her alone." Joey and Knight Walker said.

"You both seem to be very much protected of her. In that case I think I might take her with us to our Dark Kingdom." Dark King said.

"You will not take her anywhere." Knight Walker said.

"Do you love her Knight Walker or should I say

Leroy Addams guardian of all four elements." Dark King said.

"How do you know me?" Leroy said.

"WHAT!" Alena and Joey said together.

"You would love to know. For now, I will take what means more to you than anything in this world." Dark King said.

"Dark Lighting; strike them down, Dark Silence; take away their voices, and Darkness take their sight." Dark King yelled.

"Now my followers bring her to me." Dark King said.

"NO!!!! It will not that easy to get me." Alena yelled.

As she is being dragged into the dark vortex or black hole. The only thing she remembers was that her friends needed her. That she may never see them again. As she is being taken into the dark vortex of the Dark King Zodiac. She landed in a throne room, where three chairs sat. She saw windows, pictures, armor with weapons. The floors were made up of solid stone, the walls had breaks for the walls, and the throne room chairs had wood she has never seen before. The throne room looked like it was very old; it was as if she had been here before. It was like that dream she had the night before. What is it with this place she could not put her finger on it.

"Welcome guardian of the Crystal Star of Water and Ice." someone said.

"Who are you, and where am I?" Alena asked.

"My father was right you are quite the beauty. You are in the Throne room of the Palace in the Dark Kingdom Zodiac. I am the price of this palace and this kingdom." The Dark Prince said.

"What is your name?" Alena asked.

"My name is Prince Jordan." Prince Jordan said.

"Tell me what your name is, guardian? How many more guardians there are?" Prince Jordan said.

"Why do you even want to know?" Alena said.

"I want to know, because if you are going to be my bride then we need your name." Prince Jordan said.

"What! I am not marring you. My name is Alena Patches, I am 15 years old." Alena said.

"The right age to marry here." Prince Jordan said.

"Don't you have someone you are truly in love with?" Alena asked.

"That don't matter, as long as the princess is not found you are the next in line because you are the first female guardian to be found." Prince Jordan said.

"Well, I got news for you friend; I am in love with someone else. I also have a boyfriend, which you cannot even amount too." Alena said.

As the two stood in the throne room talking about what was going to happen. Alena was starting to get worried about Joey and Leroy. She hoped they would be fine and find a way to get her out of this mess. Meanwhile the other two guardians were recovering from the attack by the Dark King. When they finally got their sight back, they were wondering around looking for Alena. As they were looking around Jennifer Muse came up to them and started to talk to them about what happened when the Dark King casted his spell on them so they could not see what had happened to her.

"This is your entire fault." Joey said.

"What do you mean this is my fault?" Leroy asked.

"If you had not came and wanted to play hero, then Alena would be safe and here with me." Joey yelled.

"You mean she would be here with me." Leroy said.

"Aren't you with Sue? How do you think this would make her feel to find out that you are into her best-friend and not her." Joey asked.

"Yes, and Alena is my friend, so I'm need her here to help to understand Sue better." Leroy said.

"You do not care about her, only if it benefits you. How can you just sit there and justified you actions." Joey said.

"YOU ARE WRONG!!" Leroy yelled.

"What do you mean?" Joey asked.

"I care about her since the day I meet her at school. I only went out with Sue to make her jealous. I like Sue a lot; she is a lot of fun; she is fun to be with, but I liked Alena when I first meet her. I cannot fright the feelings I am having for her anymore." Leroy said.

"You finally admit that you care about her, and more than just being friends. Sorry we are going out and I do not plan to break up with her any time soon. She is one of a kind." Joey said.

"You are right she is one of a kind. She is full of life, happiness, friendship, and she would risk her own life to help those she cares about." Leroy said with tears, and a sad face.

"You, two need to quick fright with each other and start to look for Alena." Jennifer said.

"She needs you two to get along now to help find her. I also need your help to find the guardian of Light and Travel so we can find all the other guardians. This guardian will help you benefit in finding Alena and saving her. IF I know the Dark King, Dark Queen, and Dark Prince then Alena may be forced into something neither one of you would want." Jennifer said.

"What would that be?" Leroy and Joey said together.

"It can mean, she might be forced to marry the Dark Prince, be force to find the princess and prince, she could be forced to fight all of the guardians, or even worst she could be killed." Jennifer said.

As they are talking Leroy could not help but worry about Alena. When do find her, he is just going to come out and tell that he likes her a lot. He will have to tell Sue that it was not meet for them to be together only friends. Ask for Joey he is going to give Leroy a problem about this. As they walk back to the shelter house to check on Sue to make sure she is finding. They find her still passed out and Leroy went over to her and wakes her up.

"Sue is you okay?" Joey and Leroy asked.

"Hun, yes, I am okay. I had this wired dream that Alena was taken by some darkness." Sue said a little confused.

"Well, she went home, because she was not feeling good, and ended up getting sick again." Joey said.

"We need to go check on her to make sure she is going to be okay." Sue said.

"It will be fine Sue, I just came from her house, and she said not to worry about her, that she will see you soon." Jennifer said.

"If you say so. I am just not sure how to handle this when people are getting hurt by this darkness." Sue replied.

They all walk Sue home, to make sure she was okay. If there is a chance that we can find this guardian of Light and Travel of the Crystal Star of Light, then maybe we have a chance to get Alena back before things turn for the worse, they were all thinking. As the boys walk home, they agreed to come to a peace so they could find Alena, find the guardian of Light and Travel, and to keep anything else form happening in the meantime.

Back at the throne room Alena could feel

the darkness around, and was very feared that something would happen to her friends and the people on her Crystal Star of Water and Ice. Even through some of the people there were not particularly friendly they still did not deserve to be enslaved by this darkness. They have the right to live their life the way they want to. What is this dark kingdom up too, why are they after people's souls, minds, and energy.

"Prince Jordan, tell me why is that you all are after minds, souls, and energy?" Alena asked.

"Do you think that people will be willing to come on their own free will? I know you are smarted than that guardian, or should I just call you Alena." Prince Jordan asked.

"I do not care what you call me. What you are doing is very wrong. People have the right to live the way they want. Not be forced to do your binding." Alena yelled.

Chapter 9

As Alena is talking to the dark prince, she noticed that there were not very many people who were around. She wonders if all the people of this dark kingdom had become enslaved by the Dark King, Dark Queen, and Dark Prince. It was just a matter of time before they force her to become one of them even if she did not want to. They would force their evil energy on her so that she would do their binding and be forced to marry someone that she did not know and worse did even love. Granted she was not in love with Joey, and cared or even loved Leroy, but this was still wrong to force someone into something that she did not want. How could anyone want to do that, or even be like that? She kept wondering. As she was wondering how she could also get herself out of this mess. Prince Jordan started to say something.

"Please take her to her room, so she can get freshened up for dinner tonight." Prince Jordan said.

"As you wish your majesty." The guards said.

As the guards show Alena to her room, the house cleaners came in to get her a new dress out. As she was looking to see what type of dress it was. She fell silent because the dress they pulled out was the same dress she had dream about days ago. Light blue, with sapphire crystals all over it, and a lace open back, which flowed down to the floor. She could not believe her eyes. Was this true or is this a dream she was having again.

"Ma'am, this once belonged to the princess of the Majestic Star Kingdom which was kept hoping one day our prince would find the princess and she would ware it again. He thinks it would suite you now that the Dark King and Dark Queen claimed you to become his wife soon." The head house cleaner said.

"It is exceptionally beautiful, but I am not going to be his wife, let alone be anything to him. The dress should go back to whom it belongs to, and I should not be a loud to ware it." Alena said.

"Well, my dear please try it on and see if it fits, and if it does not then we will find a dress more to your liking. It is our job to make sure you are well taken care of until the wedding date is set." The head house cleaner said.

"Okay, I will try it on, only because you ask so nicely." Alena said.

As Alena is trying on the dress, she realized it fit to a "T" and that it did make her hair, and skin tone stand out. As she was looking in the mirror, she notices that she looked very pretty in the dress, but it would not matter if she cannot show it to the one guy she cares about. As she is staring at her reflection in the mirror she started to cry, because she wanted so badly to show it to Leroy, Sue, and Joey which are her friends. All she wanted to do was go home and be with them so much that her heart ached. As she is standing there looking at the mirror, she turns around to get a better look, and thinks no I cannot ware this dress.

"I'm sorry the dress does not fit it is too tight." Alena said.

"Oh, I'm sorry about that, because it would look really great on you." The head house cleaner said.

"Will you please find me a dress that is pink, with ruffles, and an open back without lace?" Alena asked.

"Yes, I think we can find you what you want." The house cleaners said together.

As the house cleaners leave the room, Alena rushed over to try and lock the door. As she is started to lock the door the Price bust into the room.

"I KNOW THIS DRESS WILL FIT YOU. SO PUT IT ON AND SHOW ME IT DOESN'T FIT." Prince Jordan yelled at Alena.

"FIRST OF; YOU CAN STOP YELLING AT ME. I'M NOT PUTTING THAT DRESS ON, AND MOST OF; NOT IN FRONT OF YOU; JERK." Alena yelled back.

As they stand in the doorway staring at each other. She was not going to stand for this from him, because she did not take this from Leroy. They hated each other with a passion, and she did not take it from the kids at school.

"First you can stop telling me what to do; I'm not your punching bag let alone anything else to you." Alena said.

"Well, if the dress doesn't fit then I will pick the dress not you." Prince Jordan said.

Price Jordan went and looked for a dress that would make her stand out, because her beauty was beyond those girls he has ever seen. The dress was going to be purple, lace in the shape of roses which is going to go up the dress; it will flow down to the ground and would shimmer so that the whole kingdom will notice her. It would also make her beauty stand out and most of all her hair would be the most noticeable thing in the ballroom. The prince was going to make sure of that. She will be on my arms the whole night, and nobody will be allowed to dance with her except him as the prince was thinking. There will be no guy that will touch her, only he will be the only one to have her, in all ways, even if it must be by force. This made the prince smile, which it had be an exceptionally long time since he first saw this girl that was more beautiful than the moon. This was close looking to Alena except she was the princess of the Majestic Star King, as his dark family approached this kingdom balcony wearing this dress that could be seen miles away and her beauty was beyond compared to those he has ever seen, except for Alena which her beauty is equal to that of the princess.

"One day when she is found again, I will make her mind, and do away with this guardian, even though her beauty is equal to that of the princess she is no princess, she is far beyond that." Prince Jordan said aloud.

As he was walking down the hall to the area, he needs to be to get the dress he was looking for he notice that he still likes what he sees in Alena, but to make her his wife someday soon would make him happy but not happy because she is not who he wants. She is close but no comparison to the princess, then as he kept walking, he stops and looks to see where he is there on the wall is a picture of the princess. Then it hit him she looks so much like the princess, but still something was missing, could she be the princess they need to take over this galaxy and the next ones, Prince Jordan was thinking. Could she be the lost princess that everyone was looking for? That was a question that will have to be answered later Prince Jordan was thinking. So, he goes into the rood were all the ballroom clothes are for guest and the dress he was looking for was there. So, he grabs the dress off the hanger and walks back to Alena's room. It took less time to walk back to the room then it did go to the dress room. As he walks into the room, she is sitting on the bed with the clothes she had on when she was taken from her star. Pants, t-shirt, sneakers on which did not much for her beauty, but you see it radiating off her.

"Here, please put this dress on, there is not much time left before the ball starts and dinner is served." Prince Jordan asked nicely.

"Fine, I will give it a shot." Alena replied.

As she is trying the dress on, it fit her loose which was fine with her because she was not trying to show her body off to this jerk or his kingdom. SO, she comes out of the bathroom to show him that the dress fit and that she would wear it for tonight only.

"It looks like it might be a little big for you." Prince Jordan said.

"You are mistaken. The dress fits fine and thank you." Alena replied.

The prince takes Alena by the arm so she can get her hair done in the little time there was left. She was wearing her hair half up and half down with curls ringing down her back, with a tiara on top of her head.

"What is this for? Why do I need to even dress up? Who am I going to impress because from where I am standing this place is a dumb." Alena asked.

"We need you to look like a princess for when we introduce you to our kingdom as the future queen of the dark kingdom." Prince Jordan said with a smirk on his face.

"WHAT?" Alena said.

"That is right. You will become my queen and

bride and bring a new age upon us with your Prowers." Prince Jordan said.

As Alena was getting her hair done and makeup done, she could not believe what she got herself into. As she sits there thinking how she could use this as her advantage to get out of here. She could not help but think about her friends, her family, and those she cares a lot about. This would be a perfect moment if it was the right person and right place. As she starts to cry about what has happened, she realized that everyone was looking at her. Then she wiped away he tears and put a smile on her face. She wanted more than anything to be happy at this moment in time but could not bring herself to do so. So, she pretended that everything was all right and that she was crying happy tears. So, the prince takes to the grand ballroom to see what it looks like. The grand ball room was exceptionally beautiful, the walls looked old as in Greek old, there was white pillars that went clear up to the top of the room, there was flowers of different kinds, chandelier made up of crystals of all colors, the ones that Alena notice more than anything was the rose color crystals that shine like pink and red roses. Some of the crystals looked like they were made up of rose shapes. It was the most beautiful thing in the whole room.

"How can something be so beautiful in a place like this?" Alena asked.

"Well, it seems to suite you very much, but it was copied from the Majestic Star Kingdom grand ball room. This is where we will be married, and the ball for tonight will be held here. This ball room has not been used in many years." Prince Jordan said.

"Oh, I see. This was copied so if the princess of this kingdom were found she would seem to be at home and remember what it was like when there was peace. Am I right?" Alena said and asked.

"You are very smart; you hit it right on the nail head." Prince Jordan said.

As the two walks around the grand ball room Alena could not help but feel as if she has been in this grand ball room before. In a past life, or something. As the two walk around for a few minutes one of the house cleaners came into the grand ball room.

"Excuse me sir. It is time for dinner." The house cleaner said.

"Okay, let us go have dinner then we will have a suitable time dancing together tonight." Prince Jordan said.

Both Prince Jordan and Alena left the grand ball room. They walked to the dining hall to have dinner. As they walk into the dining hall it is filled with a lot of people. As Alena could see there was nowhere to sit, then she notices to empty chairs at the main table with the Queen and King. So, she went with the prince and sat down, to eat.

Chapter 10

As Alena sits at this table in front of the whole Dark Kingdom, she could not help but cringe at the looks she was getting from these people. What was going on why did these people hate her, what is it they wanted from her, and why she even wondering? Well, she was not going to give them the satisfaction of making her feel out of place or even a part of this kingdom she was going to get out of here in one way or another. So, she was not going to eat much, she was not going to dance with the prince tonight, she plains on getting out of here. So, she started plain her escape from the Dark Kingdom.

Meanwhile on the Crystal Star of Water and Ice. Joey and Leroy were planning to get Alena out of that dark place and bring her back home. They were not going to let her stay there without any help from her friends. As Jennifer was walking up to the boys at school, she notices that the other protector had been waiting for her.

"What is it?" Jenny asked.

"I found out who the guardian of light and travel is." Male protected said.

"Who is it?" Jenny said.

"First let us get to the other guardians and talk." Glen Jones said.

"Okay, but you must know that the dark kingdom has taken Alena." Jenny said.

"WHAT! Why didn't you notify me before now?" Glen said.

"I have been with two of the other guardians and trying to figure out a plan to save her." Jenny said.

"Okay." Glen said.

As the two protectors walk over to both the boys. They sat down with them to start talking about how to save Alena.

"Leroy, this is Glen another protector from the Majestic Star Kingdom." Jenny said.

"Glen this is Leroy the guardian that has the power over all four elements, the guardian of the Crystal Star of Elements. You remember Joey right." Jenny said and asked.

"It is nice to meet you Leroy and welcome to the team. It is good to see you are doing well Joey." Glen said.

"Who is the guardian of light and travel?" Jenny asked.

"She is none other than your friend Sue Stang. She is the guardian of the Crystal Star of Light." Glen said.

As Glen is telling the two guardians and Jennifer

about whom the guardian of light and travel is. He was shocked to see that they were not surprised about this news. As he looks at them, he starts to wonder if they might have gone into shock and lost the ability to speak.

"Did you not hear me?" Glen said.

"We heard you. It is not much of a surprise that she is it when she can control light. Alena expected she might be one as well." Joey, Leroy, and Jenny said together.

"If you notice something strange, why did not you tell me. We are a team that needs to learn to trust each other and work as one. Each of us has a weakness and a strength." Glen said.

"We were not a 100% sure she was a guardian, even more the guardian of light and travel." Joey said.

"Now that it has been confirmed. How will you tell her?" Glean asked.

"Not sure yet how to tell her. It will have to be soon because we need her abilities to save Alena." Leroy said.

"First thing we need to do is find her." Joey said.

"Leroy, when you go into first period asks Sue to meet you after school." Joey suggested.

"Okay. What are you two going to do?" Leroy asked.

"We are going to in role as third formers in your school." Jenny said.

"That will be great." Leroy and Joey said together.

As the four walks into school for first period Leroy starts looking for Sue. He finds her talking with some other classmates until the bell rings for first period. He walks up to her and starts to talk to her.

"Sorry for interrupting. Sue, can I have a word for a minute." Leroy said.

"Sure, what is going on?" Sue asked.

"Nothing, I just wanted you to meet me after school today so we can have some time to get to know each other better." Leroy said with a smile.

"Okay, I can meet you after school. I was going to go over and see Alena to see how she was doing, but I will have to go later then." Sue replied.

"Um, I was hoping we could spend the afternoon together." Leroy said.

"I would love to, but I want to check on my best friend." Sue said.

"I know, but can't you call her tonight after we spend time together." Leroy suggested.

"I guess I can, because it seems to be very important to you to want to spend time together and talk." Sue said.

"Yeah, I would really love that. Thank you." Leroy said.

"You are welcome." Sue said.

Then Sue went back to talking with the other girls when the bell finally rang for first period to start. Ms. Jones was in a very good mood today she starts the class off with a free time, and then she had them to open their schoolbooks to page 586. This was the first time they were reading poems in class since it was a safe way to start a great lesson off. The whole class enjoying it so far.

"Now class we will be writing our own poems over the next few weeks of class." Ms. Jones said.

The whole like this idea because it met that there would be little homework going home. So, the class started on their first poems.

"Class please starts writing your poems today and there will be no homework after school." Ms. Jones said.

"Leroy will you please start us off." Ms. Jones asked.

"Roses are red, Violets are blue, Sue you are so sweet, there is no friend like you." Leroy said.

When he was done Sue started to blush and her face turned red. She could not help but smile because it was nice.

"Sue, will you please read your poem you wrote." Ms. Jones asked.

"Stay with me my true love; I need you now and again; stay with me my true love; you know you are my only love." Sue said.

As the rest of the class had read the poems, they wrote aloud to the class, by the time everyone had finished the class bell rang for sound period. As Leroy and Sue walk to the gym they met up with Joey and as they are walking to gym class, they run into none other than Jennifer, and Glen. They stop and talk for a minute to them.

"Hi Glen, Jennifer." Leroy and Joey said together.

"Hi Glen, how have you been?" Sue asked.

"It has been a while since I see you, Sue. I have been good; I just started school here today." Glen said.

"You have met." Jennifer said.

"Yeah." Glen said.

"It is nice to see you again Sue." Jennifer said.

"It has been awhile Jenny." Sue said.

As they are standing in the hall talking to each other the bell rang for class to start. So, everyone had to run to their next class to make it on time. As they enter, they notice that no one has started to play basketball which is what they were working on this quarter. They go in sit down on the bench next to a few classmates.

"Well class we will not be having class today. There is an assembly getting ready to start and we are all going to sit through it. So please take sit anywhere that is comfortable to you, because the assembly will be exceptionally long taking over at least three periods." Coach said.

"Well, that explains what is going with gym class." Leroy said.

"Yeah." Sue and Joey said together.

The three friends took sits on top of the bleachers so they can be left alone while they have a chance to talk to each. While Leroy was debating whether to tell Sue now about being a guardian who should be good; because there will not be anyone listening to them talk as the assembly is going on or should he still wait until after school. As Leroy was debating whether to tell her; Jennifer and Glen walk up to the three friends.

"Hey, Leroy are you going to tell her now?" Glen asked.

"I'm not sure if I should tell her now or wait?" Leroy said.

"I believe that it is an enjoyable time to at least try." Jenny said.

"Okay, here goes." Leroy said.

"Hey Sue, I think we can talk now with the assembly going on." Leroy said

"Okay, what did you want to talk about?" Sue asked.

"I know about you having extraordinary gifts and so does Alena. It is hard not to notice when Alena and you tend to disappear at times. It is okay because I am a guardian as well." Leroy said.

"But how did you find out?" Sue replied.

"I need to tell you something about myself that you should know." Leroy said.

Chapter 11

"What is it?" Sue said.

"Well, you see have a gift to control all the elements and I am not really from a faraway country, I come from a whole another place. See my home is a different Crystal Star system. My home planet is called The Crystal Star of the Elements. It is the same for you as well Sue. You are a guardian just like Alena, Joey, and me. Which would mean Joey is not really your cousin." Leroy told Sue.

"WHAT ARE YOU TALKING ABOUT?" Sue yelled but could not be heard over the assembly.

"Sue you are a guardian that is supposed to protect our prince and princess. You are the guardian of Light and Travel. Jennifer and Glen are our protectors to help us grow and get stronger to find our princess and her true love the prince." Leroy explained.

"I am not a guardian about which you are talking. Yes, I have extraordinary gifts, but I was not adopted. So, you are mistaken." Sue said.

"We were reborn on our own planets. I know that you were reborn here with Alena. This is Alena's home star planet." Leroy said.

"I do not care what you are saying. It cannot be true." Sue said.

As Sue sits there listening to Leroy the others had chimed in to help her understand. As they are sitting it starts to get dark, and the whole school was in the gym started to fall asleep, expect the five sitting together.

"I see that there are guardians here from the Majestic Star Kingdom." Strange Voice said.

"Which one of you is Alena the guardian of the Crystal Star of Water and Ice." Strange Voice said.

"You should know that she is not here that your dark king took her for his own selfless needs." Joey and Leroy yelled.

"The guardian has two men that love her. I am here to tell all you guardians that she will become mine." The Dark Prince Jordan said.

"So dark prince you plain on making her yours with control." Leroy said.

"Why did you take her?" Sue asked.

"Because guardian of light and travel she was the next in line to marry me if the princess was never found or will never be found if the Dark Kingdom Zodiac has anything to do with it. The Majestic Star Kingdom will never be reborn if the princess does not marry the prince of the Crystal Star of the

Elements. Is not that right Leroy, or should I say your highness." Prince Jordan said.

"What do you mean? You have lost it. You are crazy if you think that I am the elemental prince that is destined to marry the star princess. That is laughable." Leroy said.

"It will seem you have not regained all your memories of your past life prince." Prince Jordan said.

"It would seem that there is no chance for you to every regain your memories unless all 12 guardians are found and in place then the princess will be revealed." Prince Jordan said.

"Unless we find all guardians then there is no chance to save this world or the other worlds?" Joey said.

"No young prince of summons. See I know more about you guardians then your protectors do. As well each is a prince and princess of their own star system, but together with the princess and prince of the Majestic Star Kingdom they make up the guardians to protect these mare humans, and the stars to keep peace. We the Dark Zodiac Kingdom want all you have and more." Prince Jordan said.

"What do you want with us? What do you want with these students?" Sue asked.

"We need them and their souls, minds, bodies, and energy to take over this mare star system and to gain more power." Prince Jordan said.

"I will not allow this to happen." Sue yelled.

"Guardian of Light and Travel you are quick beautiful, but you are not in the lead of the princess or the Guardian of Water and Ice." Prince Jordan said.

"I do not care if I am in the same lead as them because I am me and they are them. I will not allow you to do as you please here." Sue said.

"Then in that case lets' see what you have." Prince Jordan said.

"Come to me dark winds of the king Dark Zodiac!" Prince Jordan said.

"NO!!!!!" Sue said.

"I call you element of wind come to me." Prince Leroy said.

"I summon you Wind Dragon." Prince Joey said.

"Listen to me Sue. You can do this; you need to so you can help your fellow classmates and your best friend. Please believe in yourself." Glen and Jennifer said together.

"I call the power of Light to me." Sue said.

Then as she notices; it had gotten very bright in the gym, and in her hand, she held a ball of light which was immensely powerful. She did not know what to do after she had called her power to her. When she looked up, she notices that Leroy was controlling the wind and that Joey was riding on the back of a Dragon the color of Blue Sapphires. The dragon was beautiful that she could not help but look at it. As she was standing there looking the dark prince had let his power go and it hit them all. She flew across the gym along with her friends. They are seemed to be very hurt. She was not going to let this dark prince get away with hurting her friends and taking her best friend away from her. She stood up and looked at him with complete discus.

"I will not let this happen." Sue said.

As her angry built up she felt so powerful that she called a ball of light to her. She throws the ball of light at the dark prince knocking him down to the ground. Then she let out another attack of light and as it hit him, she notices he was getting weaker. So, she kept hitting him with her power. When she felt completely out of energy she fell to the floor, and she became unconscious then her friends got up and hit the prince with all they had.

"This is not the last time you guardians will hear from me. I will be back to get my revenge on all of you. Alena Guardian of water ice and Princess of the Crystal Star of Water and Ice; only has until this weekend, and she then will become my wife and her powers will be mine." Prince Jordan said.

As the prince disappeared the guardians got up and watched as the students started to wake up from being unconscious. As the students came to, they notice that it was time to go home for the day. As the bell rang Sue ran out of the gym crying because she did not want to believe that she was not who she was. She wanted to go home and talk to her parents and ask them if she was their daughter by blood. As she ran out of the gym Leroy and Joey went after her but were stopped by Jennifer and Glen.

"What is going on here? Let us get her and make sure she is, okay?" Leroy and Joey said together.

"It is best to leave her alone for a little while. So, she can understand what is going on and to get answer that she needs. You two need to start planning on how to save Alena with or without Sue's help; Okay." Jennifer said.

"Fine." The boys said together.

As they watch Sue run out of the gym, they stayed were they were so that they do not cause any more heart ache or pain for her. She did need time to get a better understanding of what is going on and that she will have to be the one to find the other guardians without their help. As the two boys start to walk out of the gym Glen and Jennifer stop them.

"Please work together to find Alena before time runs out for her and us." The protectors said together.

The boys spent time together today to start planning to save Alena with and without Sue's help.

➤┤◆➤┤◆O◆┤◆┤◄

Meanwhile Sue is walking home, and she runs into the guy she saw earlier that day. She stopped and watched him as he went into a store and came out with someone by his side. She wanted so much to walk up and talk to him. She knew he was at a first-year college student, and he was particularly good looking. She also did not want to think about what happened today at school. She wanted to forget all about it. What she could not forget was the fact that her best friend was in trouble, and she needed her. As she stared off into space with everything going through her head. She gets knocked down by someone. When she looks up, she realized it was him.

"Are you all, right?" The handsome guy said.

"Yeah, I just spaced out. I do not normally to that. I just got a lot on my mind. You do not to know that." Sue said bushing.

"Someone as you, and you are having guy problems? Are you having friend problems?" The handsome guy asked.

"Well, it is nice to see you again my dear." Andrew said.

"It is nice to see you, Andrew." Sue said.

"Why don't we walk and talk." Andrew said.

"Okay." Sue said.

Andrew and Sue walked on down the sidewalk. They started to talk, and Sue could not believe that this guy as handsome as he is wanted to talk to her. She knew she was very pretty, but why would any guy in his lead and a college student to boot. All she could do was keep talking about what happened to her at school. She did not tell Andrew she had a boyfriend her age. She did on the other hand tell him about her day at school, but something told her not to tell him about what truly happened. So, she bent the truth a little to make it sound like her and her friends had an agreement. So, she just kept talking to him and she was wondering why he wanted to sit there and listen to her ramble about normal teenage things.

Chapter 12

———◦———

"Why do you want to listen to a teenage girl ramble about her school?" Sue asked. The man was standing by a water fountain that had some type of create on it. It is made up of amethyst, marble, quarts, and gold rose.

"Well; I like you, and I like to listen to you talk. It is always nice to meet someone who is a great person in general." Andrew said.

Sue was shocked to hear that he did not mind listening to her in fact he enjoyed listening to her ramble about what went on in her life. A guy she only met a few days ago seemed to be extremely interested in her. She was wondering why she felt so comfortable and complete whenever she ran into him. She had only talked to him once and it felt so right that if she did not get to see him again, she would not be able to breathe without him running into her every so often.

"Andrew was that girl that was with you your

girlfriend?" Sue asked with a hint of jealousy in her voice.

"She is not my girlfriend she is just a good friend that helps me out with schoolwork. She is in one of my study groups at school and after school. So please do not be jealous too much, the only one that I have notice around this small city is you." Andrew said with a little laugh.

As Sue and Andrew sat there on the bench across from the fountain; Sue could not help but wonder if Andrew was her destiny. The fountain was exceptionally beautiful it was made of white marble, flowers all around it, with a fairy holding a vase that is pouring out the water like pixy dust. Andrew was happy to be sitting here with Sue even though he knew she was too young for him, but he could not help but want to be near her even more now than the first time they met by share accident.

"Sue, would you mind if he could start hanging out with each other after you get out of school?" Andrew asked.

"WHAT!!! You, Andrew a college student wants to hang out with a second former in High School?" Sue asked with surprise

"Yeah, I want to get to know you a whole lot better. I think that we can be good friends. OH, I am so sorry you do not want to hang out with a college guy over your friends, you already have a boyfriend that gets all your attention." Andrew said with a sad face.

"No, that would be cool to hang with you, would it be okay if my friends hang with us too? I think that you could help us with our schoolwork if you have the time." Sue said.

"That will be fine with me. I would like to meet your friends." Andrew said.

As the two sat there talking about anything and everything. Andrew could not help keeping looking at her. She was the most beautiful woman he has ever seen. He wanted to get to know her much better; he wanted to know everything about her. Her skin is so beautiful; her hair was down to her waist, and blonde or golden as the sun. So, she sat there listening to her and watching her every move. Sue was happy that someone wanted to listen to her for once. He was tall, skin white as a cream color wall, hair was down to his shoulders and dark as the bark of a tree, and his eyes were so deep blue as the sea. Shea wanted nothing more than just to sit here and watch him. So, they sat and talked until it started to get dark.

"Well, I need to get home before my parents start to worry about where I am." Sue said.

"Let me walk you home so that you don't get hurt." Andrew said.

"Okay that sounds like a really promising idea." Sue said.

The two started to walk to Sue's house, and they start to pass the park Sue felt very uneasy like a dream had happened here the other day when she woke up on a bench at the park when her friends and her were having a study group so they can get their project done. Then something odd had happened she felt sleepy, and she fell asleep while doing her project. Then it hit her she could not believe what happened today at school happened the other day at the park. So, her being the guardian of Light and Travel that would make her a strong guardian because the others mentioned that they needed her to save her best friend Alena who happens to be in some major trouble. So, she would have to save her best friend while trying to keep a low profile. As they walked up to her house, she notices Andrew was staring at her.

"Well thanks for walking me home." Sue said.

"You are very welcome. Where were you a minute ago because you were out in space?" Andrew asked.

"Oh, you noticed. I was thinking about school and how we did on our group school project." Sue said.

"Oh, I see. So, you had a project and was wondering how you and your friends did." Andrew replied.

"Yeah." Sue replied.

As she was getting ready to walk into her house Andrew grabbed her by the arm and pulled her into a hug and held her there for what seemed like forever. She did not want to let him go, but she notices the air seemed to get warm around them. She looked up and Andrew bent down and kissed her on her rosy, red lips. In the shadow there was an image of someone. When she realized who it was, she felt bad about the kiss and hug. She pushed Andrew away and blushed about the kiss.

"You look very friendly. You know your way around here and it helps to be able to learn from you." Leroy said with angrier.

"Ummmmm." Was all Sue could say.

"Hi, I am sorry about that I could not help myself. She is exceptionally beautiful. You must be Sue's boyfriend." Andrew said with a smirk.

"Hi Andrew, I am Leroy. Yes, I am her boyfriend." Leroy said with angrier.

"Look man I did not mean any harm in it. She has been with me all afternoon." Andrew said with a huge smile.

"Yeah, I know because we were supposed to meet up this afternoon after school. I know why she did not show up." Leroy said.

"I am so sorry Leroy, I did not mean to forget, and I did not mean to hurt you like this. It just happened. Please do not be to mad." Sue said.

"Well, let me guess that we are over. Also, we needed to still talk about what happened today." Leroy said.

"Okay, I understand what happened and I get the feeling that it is far from being over." Sue said.

Andrew looked between the friends and was completely confused about what happened at school, and what is going on right now. As he stands there watching the two friends, he notices that the air got hot and hard to breathe in. Then out of know where a dark fire ball hit them and sent them all flying into the air. Then Sue and Leroy look around to see where the fire ball came from. As they look up over her house, they see something very dark and storming. She ran into her house to find her parents knocked out on the floor.

"WHAT IS GOING ON?" Sue yelled and started to cry.

"This is my family. How could this happen." Sue asked.

"It happens to the best of us." Leroy said.

"Who is here?" Leroy demeaned.

"Well guardians, it would seem that my dark fire ball didn't kill you." Mystery voice said.

"Well, you must be one of the weaker generals in the Dark Kingdom Zodiac." Leroy said.

"Well young prince it would seem I have what you want. She is exceptionally beautiful and pretty." Mystery voice said.

"If you want her back follow me into my dark realm." Mystery voice said.

"Well, it would seem I made it in time." Joey said.

"You are late." Leroy said.

"Sorry dude you left me behind, so I had found a way to catch up to you." Joey said with a smile.

"So, what are we going to do?" Joey asked.

"We are all going to follower this person into the

whole to the Dark Kingdom Zodiac." Leroy and Sue said together.

"What about my family and Andrew?" Sue asked.

"They will be fine." Joey said.

"It is us they want. We need to go save Alena and let us take their invitation to come for a visit." Joey said with way to much happiness.

The three friends follow the mystery person into the dark whole to the Dark Kingdom Zodiac. As they fly through the dark whole, they land in a field that was nothing but dust and runes. It seemed the place they landed was very unhappy and wanted nothing more than to live again.

"Where are we?" Sue asked.

"My dear guardian of Light and Travel and Princess of the Crystal Star of Light and Travel. You are in the desert of the Dark Kingdom Zodiac. Our kingdom was nice once until your princess' parents took that away from us. Yes, all we wanted to do was take over everything and rule all, but the Queen and King of the Majestic Star Kingdom stopped us. So, we took what was more important to the guardians and the Queen and King was their most loved princess." Mystery voice said.

"So, you want to take away our friend, and make her yours?" Sue asked.

"No, the Prince wants her as his bride so he can take her powers and leave her near her death bed." Mystery voice said.

"Who are you? The prince's massager? So where

is your worthless prince? He too much of a coward to face us or even let our friend go?" Sue asked.

"I am one of the generals in the Dark Kingdom Zodiac's army. They call me Joan Fire. I control the power of dark fire and dark ice fire." Joan said.

"Do you even have a plan to stop us here or are you going to let us go. Either way you will regret it in time." Sue asked.

"I believe that I will kill you here and now. That way my dear dark prince will finally notice me." Joan said.

"Ice Fire comes to me." Joan said.

"Water comes to me." Leroy said.

"Water Dragon, I summon you." Joey said.

"Light Ball I call you to me." Sue said.

As the three friends let their powers go into one attack against Joan the general of dark fire and dark ice fire. As the attack hit her, she was taking away by just the force of the attack alone. It happened to be that her weakness was water and light because of her dark fire and her dark power. Hopefully, this will be the last of them for a while until can at least find Alena and bring her home. Well with the protectors still on the Crystal Star of Water and Ice. The guardians need to find their way and consider this a test for the guardians to see how powerful they have become.

"I think we need to at least locate the palace so we can find our way." Joey said.

"Yeah." Sue and Leroy said together.

Off in the distance the three guardians that notice a banded town. So, they start to walk to it hoping that there will be someone there that is nice enough to help them out or at least point them in the right direction. As the guardians are walking, they notice that the land scape is in a bad way.

"How could anyone live in a place like this. It is so unhappy and very depressing. There is no type of life in this place." Sue said with a sad face.

"Yeah, but we need to worry about the task at hand right now. Then we can worry about how depressing the place is." Leroy said.

"Yeah, we need to worry about how we can save Alena. Sue, can you use your travel power yet?" Joey said.

"I do not know. Remember I just found out that I am the guardian of light and travel. I think that if the time comes, I could tap into that power if it comes to it." Sue answered.

The three guardians had been walking in silence for what seemed a long time until they were getting closer to the town. The friends walked in this dark realm they knew that there could be an attack around every corner, so they treaded slowly. As they got closer to the town, they started to feel very uneasy about this. They knew they had to do this so they can save their friend. As they start to enter the town things seemed to be very unsteady and very unsafe to be traveling. They also knew they were started to get tried and needed to rest. So, they scan the town to find a place they could stay for a little while so they could rest. As they look, they come across a house that was giving off some light. They notice the light when they enter the town and they wanted so badly to knock on the door. So, Leroy got the nerve up to do so.

"Hello, is anyone in there? We will not hurt you we just need a place to stay for the night. We just want to get out of the rain and cold please." Leroy yelled.

"GO AWAY!!! We do not want your kind here." Strange person said.

"Please! We will not hurt you we come from a different place, and we need a place to stay to rest just for a little while and directions to the palace." Sue pleaded.

"Let's go." Joey said.

"No! We need their help." Leroy and Sue said together.

"PLEASE!!!! Can you at least point us in the right direction?" Sue said.

"What is it that you want from the palace? Why are you even here?" Strange person said.

"We need to save our friend, and we did not come here by choice. It would be so much easier if you just opened the door so we can talk." Joey said.

As the three friend's stair at each other hoping they got through to the person on the other side of the door. They choose to start to walk away when the door opened. Standing in the doorway which was cracked open only a little bit a little child was looking at them. He feared something or someone.

"I am sorry my grandmother is extremely ill; she is not like this all the time. She is just a feared if she helps someone she will be turned into a slave or dust by these dark people." The child said.

"We are deeply sorry that we bothered you and your family. We will be going then because we do not want to cause any problems for anyone; we just want to get our friend back." Sue said.

"Please do come in young ones." Strange voice came from behind the door.

"We thank you very much." Joey said.

"Hi, my name is Joseph Ryan, this is Leroy Addams, and this is Sue Stang." Joey said.

"It is nice to meet you and your friends. There are not many young people who have manners like yourself. This is my grandson Jamaal Owens, and I am his grandmother Anna. You may call me Grandma Anna." Grandma Anna said.

Chapter 13

"Welcome to our home. We do not have much, but we do have you are more than welcome to." Grandma Anna said.

"We thank you for your help." Sue said.

"Why don't we sit down, and I tell you a story about our Kingdom." Grandma Anna said.

"That will be great." Leroy said.

As the three guardians take a sit while little Jamaal gets them some food and drinks. Grandma Anna starts to tell them about the Dark Kingdom Zodiac.

"In the old times our kingdom was free, and incredibly happy. We could enjoy all kinds of things that would now be hard to get it. There was magic, music, parties, laughing, dancing, until the new ruler came to the throne. He was power hungry; he wanted all kinds of powers so he took from his own kingdom so that he could live for a long time. When there was no power left in his own kingdom, he married a beautiful woman who was noticeably young and liked what he offered her. So, they married and the two ruled over this land and took control of her own land which was a Star that was more beautiful than a person could imagine. It had waterfalls, flowers, blue skies as far as the eyes could see. The Star Kingdom was the Indigo Star system that had power over the weather. The people could make it rain at will if they were having a dreadful day, they could make it cold if they were hurt so bad, and the king wanted this power and now he has it. For the Dark Kingdom Zodiac, it was a special Star it had power of all kinds. Everyone lived in peace until the king got power hungry. So, all the peace was taken away and given to the Dark King. If a person refused to do so they would become his slaves, and those who gave their power willing became his most loyal servants. Those who serve the King, and the Kingdom were granted unbelievable power." Grandma Anna said.

As the friends sat and listened to Grandma Anna, they started to feel sleepy and before they knew it, they had fallen asleep in her living room. When the friends came too, they woke up in a dungeon that was wet, cold, damp, and smelled bad. When they finally got their minds working again, they could not believe they fell into the enemy's trap.

"Welcome to the dungeon of the palace. Your friend is here, and she is having the time of her life." Joan Fire said.

"YOU LIE." Leroy yelled.

"Young prince if only you could see how happy she is here. Would you consider joining us and giving our great prince, king, and queen your powers?" Joan said.

"Never in a million years will we join you or give up our powers to the likes of you." Sue said with angry.

"Well young guardian of light and travel it would seem that you have lost your friend to us." Joan said.

"I have not. She is not on your side. She never will be." Sue, Leroy, and Joey said together.

⊱─◈─○─◈─⊰

As Alena is still eating at the dining table someone rushes in to talk to the prince in whispers. She could not understand what was being said but she did catch a little of what was being said. Some strange people came to the Dark Kingdom Zodiac. What got her was the prince did not seem happy with this news. Could it be her friends, have they come to save her? She was wondering and hoping that her feelings were right and that they were here to help her out. But how? She wondering did they get caught in an enemy trap and so easily? Where are her friends now if they are here? All of this was running through Alena's head when she notices that the music had started up. The prince walked over to her and put out his hand to her.

"May I have this dance?" Prince Jordan said.

"No, you may not. May I retire to my room please; I do not want to be put on display for your little fantasy." Alena asked.

"No, you will stay here until the last person leaves this ballroom." Prince Jordan said.

"I can see why your servants cannot stand you. You are cold clear to the core of your own soul." Alena said.

As Alena and the prince danced the night away watching as each person left bowing to them, she could see dislike in their faces and how sad they feel. This is what it is like to be power hungry. I will never be like that Alena was thinking. She hated the fact that she is being forced to do something she did not want to do. As soon as the last person left, she pulled away from the prince and ran for the room she was given. ON her way to the room, she stopped and looked at the picture of the princess from the Majestic Star Kingdom. She could not believe that they looked so much alike. Then she over herd the house cleaners talking about some people were brought into the castle knocked out.

"They were not from here, but they had some kind of power." The first house cleaner said.

"Oh, really. Did they seem out of place?" Second house cleaner asked.

"Excuse me but do you know where these people two boys?" Alena asked.

"Yes, there were two boys and a girl." Second house cleaner said.

"Girl? What did this girl look like?" Alena asked.

"She was very young about your age, she had blonde hair, fair skin, and she looked like she might be thin and tall." First house cleaner said.

"Thank you so much. Do you know where they were taken too?" Alena asked again.

"Yeah, they were taken down to the dungeon." Second house cleaner said.

"Thank you so much, that really helps. Where are the dungeons located?" Alena asked.

"On the other side of the castle." Second house cleaner said.

"Is there any way you can show me please" Alena begged.

"Yeah, we can show. It gives us a break from all the work that yet must be done in the castle." First and second house cleaner said.

The house cleaners showed Alena to the door to the dungeons, and she followed the hall wall done the dungeons and she came to a cell where people were, but she could not see who is. So, she took a chance and asked.

"Joey and Leroy are that you?" Alena asked.

"Yeah, we knew they were lying about you are joining them." Leroy said.

"Who is all with you two?" Alena asked.

"It is me, Alena. I am glad you are okay." Sue said.

"OH, MY, GOD!! SUE!!! You are a guardian too?" Alena said and asked.

"Yeah, I'm the guardian of light and travel." Sue answered.

"That is soooooo cool!!!!" Alena said with a squeaked.

"Yeah. I am happy to see you are okay too. So which guardian are you?" Sue asked.

"I am the guardian of water and ice. Please stand back I am going to try and get all of you out. Joey or Leroy can either of you use your powers?" Alena asked.

"No, we are drained of our powers they took what they could, but Sue can still use her powers." Joey answered.

"Okay Sue light the cell so I can see the bars, and if I use my ice power maybe we can break them with our strength alone." Alena said.

"OKAY!!" Sue said with enthusiasm.

"Light come to me." Sue yelled.

"Ice come to me." Alena yelled.

As Alena uses her ice power on the bars while Sue lights the cell, they work together to break the metal bars on the cell doors. As soon as Leroy and Joey make their finally pass with a kick to the bars. They break and all the friends hugged each other and ran out of the dungeon together. As they leave the dungeons their powers start to return to them because of the palace being filled with powers.

"How dare you break out of your cell? Guardian of Water and Ice so you choose to help your friends and denned our beloved Dark Prince." Joan said.

"Whoever you are there is no way I will ever join your team and how you treat people? Everyone has the right to be free, live the way they want to, they have the right to be human." Alena said with angry.

"I will stop you were you stand!!" Joan said.

"DARK ICE FIRE COME TO ME AND DESTORY THE GUARDIAN OF WATER AND ICE!!!!!!" Joan yelled.

As the dark ice fire is aimed at Alena, Leroy knocks her out of the way to protect her, and this time he was missed too. As she is looking at him, he smiles at her and was glad that she was okay.

"Are you okay?" Leroy asked.

"Yeah, thanks to you yet again." Alena said with a smile.

Sue and Joey both could see the love they have for each other and knew they are met to be together. Joey knew this was not the time to say anything they needed to get out of here.

"I summon the water dragon!" Joey said.

"I call water to me." Alena said.

"I call light to me." Sue said.

"I call wind to me." Leroy said.

As the light ball weaken Joan, the water dragon hit her with water bombs, and Leroy and Alena caused a water vortex and as the dark ice fire hit the water it went out, hit Joan killing her on the spot. When everything cleared there stood the Dark Prince of the Dark Kingdom Zodiac.

"I go to your room and find it empty. Here you

went down to the dungeons to free your friends from my hands." Prince Jordan said.

"THAT IS RIGHT. YOU WILL NEVER UNDERSTAND WHAT FRIENDSHIP MEANS TO SOMEONE BECAUSE YOU HAVE NO HEART!!!!!!!!" Alena yelled at the dark prince.

"So, you choose these two worthless guardian guys over me who could give you all the stars in the star solar system. All the powers of which you could dream." Prince Jordan said with angry.

"THAT IS RIGHT. I CHOOSE THEM OVER YOU ANY DAY OF THE WEEK, MONTH, YEAR, OR THOUGHOUT THE WHOLE STAR SOLAR SYSTEM. THEY ARE NOT WORTHLESS, YOU ARE WORTHLESS. THEY MEAN MORE TO ME THAN YOU WILL EVER MEAN TO ME!!!!!!!!!!!!!!!!!!" Alena yelled back.

"Then so be it. I will kill them in front of you then kill you." Prince Jordan said with a smirk. Sue stood up and fought against the power overwhelming her.

"NOT IF I CAN HELP IT!!!!!" Sue yelled.

"I call travel to me; please open a worm whole to the park so I can save my friends." Sue yelled.

As she was standing there a worm whole of Light Star power opened for them all to go through. As the prince tried to grab Alena again but was stopped by the Light Star Power. As they went through the worm whole the prince was so mad that the whole Dark Kingdom Zodiac shook. As the friend's land on the grass of the Water and Ice Star. When they looked up, they knew they were home and freed from the Dark Kingdom Zodiac.

"What time is it?" Sue wondered aloud.

"Let us ask someone." Alena said.

"Welcome back you four guardians''." Jennifer said.

"JENNY you are okay and have returned to us safely!!!" Alena yelled and hugged her.

"It is nice to see you too. I see you all made it back unharmed." Glean said.

"Who are you?" Alena asked.

"Sorry Alena let me introduce you to the other protector. This is Glean." Jenny said.

"Alena it is nice to meet you finally." Glean said.

"It is nice to meet you as well." Alena said.

"What time is the dance? Will it be okay for us to attend?" Leroy asked this time.

"It will do you all some good to have some normalcy before the big battle. The dance is 7pm Friday night." Glean and Jenny said together.

"Tomorrow is the dance for school. I have been gone for days. It felt like weeks or even months in the Dark Kingdom Zodiac." Alena said.

"Yeah, well that could be that the Dark Kingdom Zodiac is so dark and colorless that it felt that long." Glean said.

The protectors and the four guardians are together for once and will be working on finding the other guardians' soon. But until it is time to look for them, they plain on going to the dance just as four friends spending time together and not as dating each other. So, the girls stop by Sue's parents' home to find they are okay, Joey and Leroy stay at Joey's house, as for the girls they stay at Alena's house to find that nothing seemed to have changed. SO, they were going to talk for a long time to each. Sue planed on telling Alena about Andrew and tell her to go for Leroy when things settle down for a while. The friends agreed to meet up at the oak tree at school around 6:30pm Saturday night.

Chapter 14

The girls were planning to stay up late and sleeping in the next day until noon. So, they could take about what has happened and what it means to be a guardian as well as to find the others. What got them was that being able to find the other guardians. The only thing that they know is it has been a long week for them. It took them days to find Alena and when it came down to, she ended up saving them in the end. Sue was able to tap into her travel power to get everyone back home safely. So, it turned out well. So, the girls went up to Alena's room to start talking.

"Sue, how do you like being a guardian?" Alena asked.

"I am not sure how I feel about it. I just found out on Monday that I was the guardian of light and travel. How do you feel about being a guardian of water and ice?" Sue said.

"I do not like the violence that goes with it. It would not have been my first choice for a career. I have been a guardian for two weeks and I am still learning things. I do have an idea on how to find the other guardians, but it would require your powers of travel and Leroy's powers of the element wind, and my power of water." Alena said.

"You do not mind it, but you are not sure about it. You do know that we must find the prince and star princess that are to become the new rulers of the Majestic Star Kingdom. RIGHT? You should also know that the prince has already been found and it is none other than Leroy Addams himself." Sue told Alena.

"WHAT!!!! Leroy is the prince that we have been looking for." Alena said.

"Yep, he is. Leroy and I broke up on Monday night due to my own fault." Sue said.

"What do you mean you broke up and it was your fault?" Alena asked.

"Well, there is this guy he is cute, and well he walked me home Monday night, and as I was getting ready to go into my house way before the Dark Kingdom Zodiac attacked. The guy bent down and kissed me on the lips, and Leroy saw the whole thing." Sue said with a guilty face.

"So, you are telling me you meet another way cuter guy than Leroy. You kiss this guy, what were you thinking? Do you know anything about this guy? Who is he? Where is he from? What is he like?" Alena asked.

"Well, I have meet him one other time when I was going to school, he ran into me by accident.

Well, I ran into him and a friend of his when I was walking home Monday after school. SO, we started to talk. When he kissed me Alena it was so magical that I thought the world had stopped spinning. It was as if time stood still just for the two us. We are met to be together. He is so sweet, nothing like Leroy's cold hard hated that he always gave you, he gave it to me that night as well. The guy's name is Andrew Whitehouse, but he likes to be called Andy." Sue replied.

"It sounds as if you really like this guy. It also sounds like he might be met for you if he can knock your socks off with just one kiss. I want to feel that someday." Alena replied.

"You will. Doesn't Joey do that for you?" Sue asked.

"No, his kisses are wonderful, but they do not take my breathe away like a true soul mate should. Do not get me wrong he is one hell of a kisser, but his kisses are not met for me, I guess." Alena replied with a sough.

"Oh, I see what you mean. Yeah, Leroy's kisses were very great, and the boy can kiss, but his was kissing me but wanted to kiss someone else. I think that someone might be the princess he is looking for, that we all are looking for not to mention the other eight guardians that we still need to find. I will tell you one thing Alena. Leroy was or is still into you quite a bit. He was from the first day you met a few weeks ago and till now." Sue said.

"Do you really think he is into me like that? I know it is a lot to ask this of you." Alena asked.

"It is not and yes, I do. He had his eye on you since he started school here. Well good night, Alena." Sue said.

"Good night, Sue." Alena said.

>-+-+>-+-O-+>-+-<

Meanwhile the boys went to Joey's house for the night. SO, they can talk about what happened and what they must do to find the princess and the other eight guardians. Joey's house was a mansion, and it had all kinds of windows in it, the pouch was tall with pillars of white with designs in it. Leroy could tell Joey had money from the way he lived. Leroy had money too, but he did not show he was rich from all aspects. Joey really did on the other hand like to show it off.

"Hey dude, instead of staring at the outside of my house, please come in and then you look at everything." Joey yelled back as he reached the front door, which was bigger than their whole front of their school.

"Sorry, man. WOW!!! Joey you are loaded." Leroy replied with a look of special on his face.

"If you think the outside is assume then you really need to check the inside out as well. I do have an extra room you can sleep in. I also have some tuxedo you can borrow if you need one for the dance tomorrow night." Joey said with a friendly face.

"That would be cool. I forgot mine at the house with everything that has happened." Leroy said.

"Well, your highness please enter my domain." Joey said with a laugh.

"That is not cool man. Please let us keep that to our self I do not want anyone to know that I was adopted and that my really family is well gone." Leroy said with a smirk on his face.

"Gotcha bro." Joey said.

"Thanks man." Leroy said.

As the two friends walk into the front room of the house Leroy took a quick look around and saw that there was a lot of art on the walls, fine China in cabinets, and a lot of high-end designer things. It was nice and yet seemed peaceful. Leroy walked over to a picture of a boy, woman, and man. In the picture the boy seemed incredibly happy and looked as if he laughed a lot. Leroy assumed it was Joey, but now he was very unhappy with the way he acts sometimes as if he is trying to hide a lot of pain from the world.

"Oh, that is a picture of my family. That is my little brother, mother, and father." Joey said with a sad look in his eyes.

"So where is your family now?" Leroy asked

"My father is a businessperson and works all the time which makes no time for me, so he gives things like this house to keep me happy. For my mother and brother, they died in a car accident right after this picture was taken. He had to been around 6 years old when this was taken." Joey said.

"Oh, I am so sorry. I did not mean to pyre." Leroy said.

"Do not worry; it has been a long time since that happened. It was around that time; that my father, and I moved away from everyone here. Including Sue, she was my escape from all the pain. Whenever I was with her; she would always find a way to keep me smiling and keep the pain away. We were at one close. Now we need to get to know each other again." Joey said.

"I am sorry this happened to you. Sue does seem to always light up the room whenever she comes in. Alena could always seem cold like ice water. Yet, she is as strong as water. Both are so different, but they are so much alike in so many ways." Leroy said.

"I know what you mean Alena can be cold sometimes like ice, and strong most of the time like water. She seems as if she has had a lot of heart ache in her past, so she pushes people away to protect herself. Sue she can be so happy in the darkest places just like light, and she can move fast as if she travels from one place to another." Joey said.

"Yeah. We know that Sue is the key to finding the other eight guardians with her ability to travel through space, but she is going to need help from all of us. Hopefully, we can find all the guardians; and the star princess will appear." Leroy said.

"I know what you mean, it would be great to find our star princess she is the key to defeating the Dark Kingdom Zodiac. We should really get some sleep it is already 3am in the morning. We do have a long day ahead of us with the dance and taking the girls. Alena and I are going to split up. So, she is free if you still want to be with her. I am not saying she is not a great person; she is too good to be true in my eyes, and she kisses as if the world were on fire." Joey said.

"I am still into her like that. I am not sure now with finding out who I am and if finding the princess means I must leave her alone so that we can regain peace. I do not want to put her through that and make her have more pain than what she has had already. What is like to kiss her?" Leroy said and asked.

"It is like kissing a girl who knows what she wants and goes after it. Her kisses are magical, mysteries, and yet they have the most warmth to them as if she could warm the world with her lips." Joey said.

"So, you enjoyed kissing her. I think that we should really get to bed." Leroy said.

"Yeah, I did. Do not act like you did not get mad when you walked into her mother's restaurant and did not get upset when you caught me kissing her for the first time. Yes, we do need to get to bed." Joey said.

"You are right I did get mad about it and even

jealousy that she would go out with you and not even give me a second looked." Leroy said.

"She gave a second looked. You had asked Sue out before even trying to ask her out. But never mind that. Good night, Bro." Joey said.

"Yeah, whatever you say. Good night, Bro." Leroy said.

As the boys walked up to the rooms. Leroy notices the halls were long and there were doors all along the hall. As Joey mad right turn Leroy followed him so that he would not get lost.

"Hey man where the room I will be sleeping in is?" Leroy asked.

"It is across from mine. Which is at the end of the hall?" Joey said.

"Cool." Leroy said.

As the boys walked along the hall, they notice that it was quite today. Joey remembered his father was out of town, and it was the maid's day off. So, they had the house to themselves. As they kept walking finally, they reached the end of the hall. Joey had turned right to the door on the right-hand side was his room, and Leroy would be staying in the room across from his which was on the left-hand side of the hall. As Leroy enter the room, he notices there was a king size bed, blue curtains, large windows that could fit a car in them easily. And a picture of the most beautiful woman he had ever seen. As he looked at the picture, he notices it had been painted by hand. The woman looked so familiar to him he could have sworn he has seen her before.

"Leroy, I hope you sleep well." Joey said.

When Joey did not get an answer from Leroy, we look to see what has his attention. Joey walks up to the painting and tells Leroy about it.

"Hey, who is that woman in the painting?" Leroy asked.

"I am not sure who she is, but she does look familiar to me. My father picked this painting up in Paris, France a few years ago and had it hung in this guess room." Joey answered.

"Oh, wow Paris, France, I have been there before. It is a wonderful place to visit. Well, I was just wondering. Night." Leroy said

"Okay, night." Joey said.

Joey went to his room and Leroy went ahead and got ready for bed in some clothes that were in the guess room dresser. He kept staring at that painting and could swear he has seen her before. As Leroy drifted off to sleep, he began to dream. The same dream he has had for many years about a girl, a kingdom, and a prince. As he slept, he realized he was the prince that was waiting for someone to come to a window that was up high. As she came to the window all he could do was stair at her. She was the most beautiful woman he has ever seen. She had hair as dark as a raven's feather which went down past her butt, skin as tan as an Indigenous person, and eyes that were light brown, to a honey color. All he wanted to do was protect her from all harm. He knew he loved her more than life itself. He would sacrifice himself for her and her kingdom if it came down to it. Then before he knew it there were guards on him.

"Who dare goes there?" Head Guard said.

"It is the Prince from the Crystal Star of the Elemental Realm." Second Guard said.

"Get him. Do not let him get away. He is a spy for the Dark Zodiac Kingdom!" Head Guard said.

Prince Leroy ran from the guards to make it out of the castle safely. He knew he had to go to the ball for which she would be there. He was invited by the King and Queen of the Majestic Star Kingdom to the ball. As the princess walks down the main staircase with her mother, she looked stunning in the grown she was wearing. She was heading to the grand ballroom. He knew he will have to dance with her just to be able to talk with his love. So, he waited in the middle of the ballroom floor until she entered the ballroom as she did everyone stopped dancing just to get a look at her. She was wearing the most beautiful grown which made her hair, skin tone, and eyes stand out. He was wearing the most handsome tuxedo a man could get.

Chapter 15

"Princess, may I have this dance? Your parents know that I am not a spy and they have asked me to help fright off the evil that is approaching the Majestic Star Kingdom Realm." Prince Leroy said. The princess took his hand. It felt warm, kindness, and love. She smiled at him that melted his heart every time she did. It was a smile that was reserved just for him.

"Will there be no peace anymore? How will we be able to stay together if the guards keep thinking you are an enemy?" Star Princess said.

"Someday and some way we will have peace again if it comes down to a fright I will fight with your parents. My army will fight alongside of this kingdom." Prince Leroy said.

"What would we do if we get separated? How will I survive? What would we do if the kingdom falls to this evil?" Star Princess.

"You are strong you have power just like your parents if not stronger than their powers. If it comes down to us separated, I will find you that is my promise to you for our love is true. I am not sure what will happen to the kingdom if it falls to this evil." Prince Leroy said.

Prince Leroy and the star princess danced the night away as if it were the last time, they ever see each other again. So, he stayed close to her just so he could hold her in his arms if this is the only protection, he can give against the Dark Kingdom Zodiac he was not going to let her go so easily. He wanted the night and peace they have for now to last forever. She felt the same way; she never wants the night to end. She hopes that the peace will last, she did not want a war to happen, most of all she wanted her family together. She wanted all her friends to be happy and have peace. As the night went on, they walked into the garden and sat on the most beautiful bench in the garden. As they sat there, they were looking at the stars and then she looks down and he is holding a ruby red rose in his hand just for her. She looked him into his dark green eyes and lend in and kissed him. She wants so bad that this would last forever, but she knew that it would not, she had the feeling things was going to bad, and it is going to last for a long time.

"Leroy wakes up." Joey said shaking him.

"What is it?" Leroy asked.

"Dude it is like 1pm in the afternoon." Joey said.

"I'm getting up." Leroy said.

As he was waking up, he had sweat coming down

his face. He knew it was not from the room being hot because it was quite comfortable, it was from the dream. He felt at peace, sad, and yet incredibly happy just to have her in his arms. She looked so familiar to him, as if he has seen her here and now. Her hair seemed so much like Alena's hair color, but they could not be the same person because Alena was the guardian of the Crystal Star Realm of Water and Ice Realm. He was going to worry about it later not right now he was looking forward to the dance and having just one dance with Alena. So, he got up and undressed and got in the shower to get clean, but he was still thinking about the kiss before Joey had woken him up. It wanted to have that kiss again someday. He had promised her that he would protect her from all harm. He said the same thing about Alena, he wanted to protect her and be near her always. He was torn between the two. He wanted to be Alena more than anything, but he made a promised to the Star Princess to be with her forever. Will he be stuck with destiny and not be happy or is it just a mare crush he has on Alena.

➤┄◄❯┄◦┄❮►┄►◄

Meanwhile the girls got up at noon, got in the shower went down and ate some lunch Alena's mother had made for them before she went to the restaurant. They started to get their hair done by each other's; Alena wore her hair up in a bun with curls hanging down in many places. Sue had curled all her hair and then pinned it up with bobby pins with curls hanging out. Then they did there make-up, so they can get their dresses on. They hoped that the boys would love the way they looked. As they were putting on the finally touches a car honked outside and it was the Limo that Alena's mom had rented for them all so that they will not have trouble getting away home if things happen.

As the girls walk down to the White Limo and get in, they start to head to the school when they knew things could go bad quite.

"Let's agree if things happen, we need to enjoy this way we can." Alena said.

"I agree with you, it may be the only peace we have." Sue agrees.

As they pulled up to the school the girls get out and walk to the middle of the courtyard where the very oak tree stood, and where they always meet after school. So, the girls waited for the boys to get there when the Limo went and picked them up from Joey's house.

The limo is white, with gold interior, a bar, some fairy lights, tinted windows, and a driver that is wearing a black suit with gold trim it pulled up to Joey's house and honked its horn and the boys came outside and got into the limo and started to talk.

"We need to enjoy this peace while we have it because anything could go wrong at any moment. With the Dark Kingdom Zodiac is going to hit hard and try everything they can to stop us from finding the other eight guardians and the star princess." Joey said.

"Yeah, we need to enjoy what peace we have because you never know when it will end." Leroy agreed.

As the limo pulled up to the school for a second time tonight it was 6:30pm and the guys were running late but had called ahead to let the girls know. As the boys start to walk over to the big old oak tree in the middle of the courtyard they stopped in their tracks and just stared at the girls. Alena was wearing the most beautiful dress ever, Sue stood out like she did not want to be missed by anyone. Alena's dress was pink with light blue trim, open lace back, with blue shimmer in the fabric, and Sue's dress was a gold dress with the V-neckline with lace going up the back, and a spilt going up the front of the right leg. Both girls looked stunning in their dresses. So, the guys walked up to them and gave them each a dozen red and pink roses.

"Thank you very much they are very beautiful." Sue and Alena said together.

Leroy is wearing a tuxedo that was light blue with gold trim going up the jacket and collar, for Joey he was wearing a black tuxedo that had light blue and pink shimmer going up the jacket and trim the collar. Both boys looked very handsome in their tuxedo, and they were very stunning.

"You both look very handsome tonight." Alena said.

"I think they look stunning." Sue said.

After complementing each other the friends walked into the gym to find it looked like a fantasy land they only had read about in books. It was homecoming dance any way. The walls were covered in fabrics of white, blue, and red. There were balloons on every table, there was a refreshment table to get drinks and snacks from, and the music was out of this world. As the friends took a table near the exit, just in case of an attack from the Dark Kingdom Zodiac. This would be a clever way to try and get them out of the gym where everyone was having a really good time. As the friends sit down the girls wanted something to drink and the boys got them a drink from the refreshment table. As the boys get back, they wanted to dance with the girls at a medium to slow song so they can enjoy this moment and the peace it offers.

"Alena, would you like to dance?" Joey asked

"I would love to dance with you." Alena said.

"Sue, would you like to dance?" Leroy asked.

"I would love to dance." Sue replied.

As the friends walk onto the dance floor everyone around stopped and could not believe that these two girls had the hottest guys in school but the most stunning dresses they had ever seen. It was uncommon for Alena to be with anyone, and Sue just came into her youth and just stood out among everyone. Alena was glad that she had a chance to dance with Joey even though she knew they would not be together as a couple but just friends which was fine with her. Sue felt the same way about Leroy she was glad that they were not a couple anymore but just friends and could get past what had happened the other day. It was a peaceful event they did not want to end. They knew that the peace will only last for so long before another attack would happen. They were just waiting for it. After they danced, they all went back and sat down to get them breathe back, and a drink before the next song came up.

"For a special request from all you on the dance floor this is a song that would bring you even closer together." The D.J. said.

The song was I Will Always Love You, By: Whitney Huston. As the song started to play Leroy bent down to Alena.

"Alena, would you honor me with this dance." Leroy said.

Alena started to giggle about it because he was being all nobble, and it did not sound right coming from him. Sue was smiling from ear to ear. Joey was not happy about it but knew that it would be oaky. So, he thought about asking Sue to dance just so they are not sitting around doing nothing but watching everyone else having fun.

"Sue, would you like to dance with me even though we are cousins. Just so we can have some fun." Joey said with a laugh.

"That sounds cool to me." Sue replied with another giggle and laugh.

They walked back out onto the dance floor and started to slow dance; and again, every stood back and just watched the four friend's dance. They could feel he warmth from them that they could not feel before. It was like someone had entered an area that was always warm and wanted to stay there and enjoy the warmth. They all could not help but smile and see the love among them. It was like they were watching a movie that was filled with love and romance. Before they knew it everyone started to feel sleeping and they could not understand why, because they were enjoying themselves. Then the friends knew why, the peace was shatter again by yet the Dark Kingdom Zodiac. As everyone had started to pass out from feeling sleepy the four guardians could fight the power of the Dark Kingdom Zodiac.

"Everyone will be mine." Cold voice said.

"Who goes there?" Leroy asked.

"Ahhhh, if it is not the prince from the Crystal Star of the Elemental Powers. It has been a long time." Cold voice said.

"Again, who are you why have you come here? Everyone was having a fun time and enjoying the dance." Alena said.

"Oh, guardian of water and ice, the Dark Prince said you were quite good looking. He was not lying one bit." Cold Voice said.

"I will destroy you for causing pain to my dear dark prince." Kane said.

"Again, what is your name?" Sue said with angry.

"Well guardian of light and travel; I am Kane dark war load of sound." Kane said.

"We will not let you do this. If you want us, then follow us." Joey said.

As the guardians ran outside to keep the students and teachers from getting hurt. The dark war load followed the four guardians into the courtyard outside the school. They set up a way to keep power of the Dark Kingdom Zodiac from causing any more problems.

"Guardians' do you plain on running away from a fight at all times." Kane said with a laugh which hurt their ears.

"We are not running away from the likes of you. We will stop you here and now." Alena said with angry.

"Let see what you have guardian of water and ice." Kane laughed.

"I call ice to me." Alena yelled.

"Sound wall." Kane yelled.

As the attack hit the sound wall it bounced back and hit Alena hard in the crest and knocking the air out of her. She did not know that would happen. They need to find a way past it.

"Are you okay Alena?" Sue asked.

"Yeah, just a little winded from the attack. We need to find a way past that sound wall." Alena said.

"Ahhhh, guardian that is not the only attack I have." Kane said.

"Sound attack spear." Kane yelled.

"EARTH WALL!!!!!" Mystery person said.

The guardians looked around to find who used that power a man stood off in the distance with his hands up controlling the earth wall. They spotted a person in the shadows and the silhouette was tall like a man. Differently to tall to be some women, at least the ones that they know.

"Guardians you can beat him all you have to do is pull your powers together. Guardian of light and travel I am not much help here you need to find all eight of us guardians that are left. Powers are not good here so I cannot hold on much longer you can find me in the Crystal Star of Earth realm, but before you can get to me you need to find three others beforehand. Also use your light rings to trap him, light is faster than sound." Mystery guy said.

Sue is confused, she has herded his voice before, but before she could get to him, he had disappeared. He said that her light was faster than his sound wave or sound wall.

"Light come to me and creates rings of light." Sue yelled.

"You can try guardian of light, but what will happen once you use your powers, can your friends help you?" Kane laughed even harder.

"Light rings trap him." Sue yelled.

"I summon the dragon of lighting." Joey said.

"Wind come to me." Leroy yelled.

"Water come to me." Alena yelled.

As the rings trapped Kane in a light rope the other used their power to defeat him. Alena used her waterpower which made it past the sound wall because Kane was trapped with the power of light, when Joey had his dragon hit him with his best lighting attack, and Leroy held the lighting in place with a tornado and when it was all done Kane had turned to dust.

"Well done guardians. You really let him have it." Glen said running up to the guardians.

"That was well played out." Jenny said.

"What is it?" Leroy asked.

"We came to tell you that at midnight tonight would be the best time to send Sue and Joey to the Crystal Star of Fire Realm." Jennifer said.

"Oh, okay. Will we have time to see who gets crowned queen and king of the homecoming dance?" Alena asked.

"Yeah, you have about 30 minutes before it is time. That is when the blood moon will appear and be at its' highest peak." Glen said.

As the guardians walk back into the dance and as they did Ms. Jones was on stage getting ready to announce who will be homecoming queen and king.

"Well gents and ladies your Homecoming Queen is Alena Patches." Ms. Jones said.

"What, I never put in for Homecoming Queen." Alena said.

"NO, I put your name in." Sue said with smile.

As Alena walks up to the stage; she was surprised that the whole school was clapping for her.

"Now for your Homecoming King: Leroy Addams." Ms. Jones said.

Leroy walked up to the stage with a huge grin on his face and he was being clapped even louder than what the whole school did for Alena.

"Here are you Homecoming Queen and King!" Ms. Jones yelled.

As they stood there their friends were in the back clapping hard for them and Joey and Sue knew that they were met to be together. They were all smiling and could not help but feel sad at the same time because two of them would be leaving this night.

"They look good, don't they?" Sue said with a tear in her eyes.

"Yeah, they do." Joey said with somewhat of a sad tone to his voice.

As the Alena and Leroy left the stage the dance was over, but for them it was completely over because they had to go to get ready to send Sue and Joey into space to find the other eight guardians.

>—+—◆>—◐—<◆—+—◁

As the friends went home long enough to change their clothes they met back at the warehouse where they trained to fright the Dark Kingdom Zodiac. Even though the warehouse was only used once for

Joey and Alena's training this was the best place to be able to open a portal to space for Sue and Joey.

"Are you ready guardians?" Jenny and Glen said together.

"Yeah." The four guardians said together.

"Alena goes ahead and start us off, Leroy joins in, Joey gets ready to summon your dragon of light, and Sue get ready to open up a portal." Glean said.

"Will we see each other again?" Alena says when she started to cry

"Yeah, remember you and Leroy have to greet the other guardians' when they come here." Sue said holding back a sob.

"Okay." Alena said.

"Let us begin." Jennifer said.

"Water come to me." Alena said.

"Wind come to me." Leroy said.

"Light Dragon, I summon you." Joey said.

"Travel I call to you to open a gate way to the Crystal Star of Fire Realm." Sue called.

"Now Alena and Leroy combined you powers into a bubble that will hold air for our friends." Jennifer said.

"Okay." Alena and Leroy said together.

"Air Bubble." Alena and Leroy said together.

"Please protect our friends." Alena said.

"Joey you and Sue need to ride the Light Dragon into the light portal and enter the Crystal Star of Fire Realm." Jennifer said.

"Okay we understand." Sue said.

As they climbed onto the dragon, they enter the light portal and as they finally see on the other side, they are in the Fire Realm. With their luck they are attack with a fire ball by a person in the distance. They fly the light dragon to a cave near to the light portal that was up high, and they could see the Fire Realm very clearly. It was a beautiful place there was red flowers, a waterfall that put off steam, mountains as far as the eyes could see. Sue wanted to keep looking and enjoy the relaxing view. She also seen a castle in the far distance just beyond the mountains.

"This is the Crystal Star Fire of the Fire Realm. It is quite beautiful. I think that we should stay here for the night until the fighting slows or comes to a stop." Sue suggested.

"I agree with you. It is one hell of a view. I never imaged that the Fire Realm was so beautiful in its own way. Then we can begin our search for the first of the eight guardians' that are left to find." Joey said.

The two set up camp and was hoping that they will be able to find the Guardian of the Crystal Star of Fire Realm. They needed more than anything to be able to show this to their friends. They knew that the plan was to find each guardian and send them back to the Crystal Star Water and Ice with messages for their friends that things were okay with them, and the search continues for the rest of the Guardians,' and the Star Princess.

The End for Now....

Printed in the United States
by Baker & Taylor Publisher Services